BOTTOM FEEDERS

BOTTOM FEEDERS

A NOVEL

JOHN SHEPPHIRD

BLACK
STONE
PUBLISHING

Copyright © 2018 by John Shepphird
Published in 2018 by Blackstone Publishing
Cover design by Kathryn Galloway English

Printed in the United States of America

First edition: 2018
ISBN 978-1-5384-6920-0
Fiction / Mystery & Detective

1 3 5 7 9 10 8 6 4 2

CIP data for this book is available
from the Library of Congress

Blackstone Publishing
31 Mistletoe Rd.
Ashland, OR 97520

www.BlackstonePublishing.com

I dedicate this novel to the legions of hard-working craftspeople and performers who have carried sandbags, set lights, cobbled together wardrobe, swung microphones, memorized dialogue, painted sets, dusted faces, pulled focus, teased hair, coordinated chaos, hit their marks, and built it all up only to tear it down again—making something out of nothing. To the dreamers and the schemers in the low-budget trenches, this is for you.

CHAPTER
ONE

It had been a year since his last cigarette—before the doctor gave Ted *the fright*. The message was loud and clear. He'd stopped smoking, tried to exercise more, and worked on eating a low-cholesterol diet. But this was fate; a half-pack of Marlboros left behind in the leather console of his rental car, a book of matches tucked snugly in the pristine cellophane. Once Ted caught the scent of the ripe tobacco—*what the hell*. This was a seductive gift from the gods. His wife would never know.

The only dilemma: there was no ashtray.

Always the problem solver, Ted fashioned a crude paper triangle out of the Hertz rental contract. Proud of his origami ingenuity, he put flame to the cig and savored the smoke, a warming sensation he hadn't experienced in a long, long time.

Ted was the vice president of sales for Artemis Industries, a pharmaceutical research firm, headed to the Advances in Immunodiagnostic Assays Conference. The sky was overcast, threatening rain, and it was getting dark. Upgraded from a midsize SUV to a luxury sport vehicle, he maneuvered the Mazda up the windy mountain road. This car had guts. It made Ted feel powerful.

Tonight, he would go through the tedious motions of pinning on his name tag, flashing his always-professional smile, and making an appearance at the welcome cocktail reception. In his midfifties and carrying more paunch then he cared to admit, Ted would suffer through the speech-laden dinner and, afterward, obligatory drinks and forced camaraderie in the hotel bar. It went with the job—employment he sensed would not last long. The batch of young salesmen among the ranks would ultimately prove to be a cheaper solution. There had already been one round of downsizing. It was the company's health insurance he needed most, for his wife's treatment. Ted long ago came to realize he was, sadly, a slave to medical benefits. With luck, maybe he could squeak out another four or five years before being forced to retire.

He *so* hated that this year's conference was up in Lake Arrowhead. The Granite Springs Hotel & Spa, for Chrissake! Did someone's fat-assed secretary pick the destination? *What the hell?* Last year the conference was at the Westin in Palm Springs, with golf, so why this sudden change in venue? More wasted time and bullshit.

Now Google Maps on his iPhone wasn't working. Bad directions had him searching for a street sign. He hadn't seen another vehicle for a while. Something told him he had taken a wrong turn.

He struck a match and was igniting a second cigarette when BAM!

The deer smashed into the windshield, cracked the glass, and flew over the top of the car. The airbag inflated into his face and he slammed the brakes. The Mazda slid sideways onto the rocky shoulder before coming to a stop.

Holy shit!

Getting out, he first heard the deer squealing before he saw the poor, wounded animal writhing on the black pavement. He examined the rental car—its grill was shattered, hood mangled, windshield fractured. There was even bloody fur caught in the satellite-radio antenna.

Fucking thing came out of nowhere.

He approached the wounded animal.

One large, glassy eye stared back at him in pure terror. It was trying to get up but its hind leg was bent back grotesquely. There was blood coming out of its mouth and it was shaking in a spasm.

Ted felt nauseous and wondered if he was going to throw up. He reached for his cell phone to dial 9-1-1. No service. *Shit.* He stepped closer. The animal's desperate whine subsided. It was now wheezing, chest heaving, struggling at the edge of death.

It broke Ted's heart. He felt incredibly guilty. *This is all my fault.* If he hadn't gone for another cigarette maybe he could have swerved to avoid the damn thing.

There was a milky secretion coming out of the deer's eyes. Tears?

Ted felt helpless and didn't know what to do. Then it came to him. *Put it out of its misery. It's the humane thing to do.*

He searched the side of the road, came across a good-sized rock. He picked it up with both hands—figured it was probably heavy enough to crush the animal's skull. As he approached, the deer tried to scramble away but its hooves gained little traction on the pavement and loose gravel.

Forgive me.

With both hands, he raised the hefty rock above his head.

That big eye stared back.

I'm sorry.

He brought the rock down. The blow was not a direct hit and the deer panicked, flopping like a fish out of water. Ted picked up the rock again and brought it down with even more force. That blow disfigured the animal's skull but it was still quivering in a violent, horrible spasm.

Shit!

Tears streaming, he picked up the rock again, hefted it high, and brought it down again with all his might. The sound was crunchy and the deer moved no more.

Finally. Thank God.

Gasping for air and now covered in sweat, Ted turned away and vomited. He could taste the cigarette in his bile.

Bent over, hands on his knees, catching his breath, he looked up, surprised to see a Ford Explorer idling forty yards up the road.

There was a faint silhouette—someone in the driver's seat.

Wiping his mouth with his sleeve, he found it odd the SUV just sat there. He wondered how much of the incident the driver had seen. Ted moved toward it, waving his arms for help.

The Explorer backed up, spun around, and was off.

Ted watched as it disappeared around the bend. Whoever it was must have seen him killing the deer—probably spooked. The only sound was the wispy wind through the trees. He tried his cell phone again. Still no reception.

Ted returned to the rental car and discovered a flat tire. He decided he better change it before it got dark. In the meantime, hopefully, someone would come along and drive him back to civilization.

He opened the trunk and lifted the carpet. He could not believe how rinky-dink the spare tire was. He retrieved the mini jack and lug wrench, and pried the plastic hubcap off. *They sure as hell don't make cars like they used to.* Moments later he had the lug nuts loose and was on one knee, struggling with the scissor jack.

That's when he heard a loud pop beside him.

An arrow stuck out of the car's quarter panel. *Arrow? Is someone hunting deer?* Then a sharp pain ripped into his back.

He spun around, reached back and felt the shaft. *Fuck!* A second arrow hit him in the chest. He grabbed that one's black carbon shaft and could feel the sharp point wedged between his ribs, an icy sensation.

Oh, God! Run.

Ted made a break for the opposite side of the road. He reached the tall weeds when the third arrow ripped into his lower back and sent him tumbling. Falling hard, he drove the other arrow deeper into his chest. He tried to scramble to his feet but somehow had lost control of his legs.

I'm going to die.

Ted tried again but his legs failed him, as if stuck in mud. Heaving, in shock, his lungs burned as he heard someone approach behind him. All he could make out was a dark figure, in silhouette, standing over the fallen deer.

He watched as the figure set down the bow and picked up the rock.

Ted crawled, tried to reach the trees. *Hide. Get away.*

Hearing footsteps near, Ted rolled back. Hands up, defensive, he eyed the silhouette and big rock raised against the murky sky.

"I didn't mean it ... I ..."

An explosion—then all went black. After the ringing in his ears faded away, he could hear a peaceful wind brushing the trees.

Then there was nothing.

CHAPTER TWO

Eddie Lyons had the routine down: wear a sports jacket, pay general admission, sneak into the Turf Club.

Just like he had many times before, Eddie waited beside the Santa Anita paddock for the outriders and jockeys to guide the exquisite Thoroughbreds into the grandstand tunnel leading out to the track. Then Eddie made his move. He blended in with the well-heeled owners and trainers and followed them to the elevators—no hand stamp required. Once inside the Turf Club, Eddie wedged up to the bar, a neutral spot that didn't require a seat ticket. Pockets loaded with airline-sized minis, he ordered a club soda and spread out his *Daily Racing Form*.

For out-of-work television director Eddie Lyons, it was going to be small bets today. Hit a few—then play with the track's money. That's the idea. "Conserving cash is the key," he'd explained to a fellow handicapper just the other day. "That's what separates the winners from the losers."

Eddie could bet and watch the races at home, or even streaming on his cell phone, but that wasn't the same. He came to Santa Anita to mix and schmooze if the opportunity presented itself. Staying in the consciousness of Hollywood power (among individuals who can green-light a project) took dedication. And sharing the passion of horse racing had proven successful for him in the past. A few years ago, an aging network executive hired Eddie to direct a television pilot after the guy hit a trifecta from a tip Eddie had offered. Unfortunately, the pilot never got picked up, and Eddie's further picks never panned out. *Story of my life.*

Besides, the racetrack was so much cheaper than Laker games, especially with Eddie's backdoor system. Sure, there were plenty of well-connected agents, stars, and executives at Laker games, but who could afford those seats? And nobody talks business when the game is in play. Horse racing is entirely different. There is plenty of time between races, socializing being such an integral part of the Sport of Kings.

When he was certain the bartender wasn't looking, Eddie poured himself a clandestine double. The sip soothed him, his first taste of the day. *All good.* Minutes later he was handicapping a maiden-claiming race on a special Columbus Day Monday card when his cell phone rang. The readout displayed a three-one-zero area code, Los Angeles, Westside. Confident it wasn't another collection agency, Eddie picked up.

"This is Ed."

"Eddie ... It's Mike Monroe."

He recognized the voice. Michael was Sam Carver's cocky, twentysomething assistant. Carver Entertainment produced made-for-television movies and they'd hired Eddie about a year ago to direct one of their cheapies, a woman-in-peril thriller shot mostly on recycled sets.

"Hey Mike. What's up?" Eddie said upbeat.

"Inquiring if you're available to come by the office today? Sam wants to see you."

"Always available for Sam," Eddie replied. Sam was an old-school producer, no nonsense, but very cheap. "What's going on?"

"He wants to talk to you about a Tami Romans thing."

Eddie knew Tami Romans—an aging actress who once starred in a popular television series. The last time Eddie saw Tami was on a late-night infomercial pitching some kind of antiaging beauty treatment.

"Tami's good," Eddie said even though he'd heard she can be difficult. *Stay positive. Get the job.* "What's the project?"

"It's kind of a *Doctor Quinn, Medicine Woman* sorta deal for Majestic Channel. Remember that show?"

"Sure."

"Sam thought of you because it's a tight schedule. Can you get here in an hour?"

Eddie checked his watch. He was certain he could make it but figured he'd build in a little time contingency so he didn't have to rush. "How about three-thirty. That work?"

"Sounds good."

"See you then."

Eddie finished his drink and grabbed his coat. *A Western?* he thought. *Cool. Majestic Channel, though? Probably kids and animals, certain hurdles on a low budget.*

As much as he regretted it, tight production schedules were Eddie's specialty. He'd built a reputation of getting the job done, always on time and under budget. Long ago he'd come to terms with the fact that he would never be recognized as an artist. He'd be known as a journeyman TV craftsman experienced in working with limited resources. "Laying pipe," was often how he described what he did as a director. It beat working in an office for a living.

Before getting on the freeway, Eddie popped into a 7-11 for Altoids and a bottle of water. He didn't want Sam to smell the Popov vodka on his breath.

* * *

Carver Entertainment was located in a Century City high-rise, and as expected, Eddie arrived sooner than he'd said. The young, sultry receptionist wearing a black leather miniskirt and zebra-print high heels escorted him to Carver's office. Eddie forced himself to not stare at her shapely legs, but damn, they were one hell of a distraction. *Be professional.*

Sam greeted Eddie with a handshake and, after the usual pleasantries, got down to business. "The picture starts right away, next week, so there's very little time," he said, taking a seat behind his vintage sixties desk. Eddie had never seen Sam wear anything other than tennis sweats and brand-new white Nikes. Today was no exception. "We're already in prep," Sam continued before adjusting the lumbar support behind his back. "Chris Sanderson was attached to direct, but we've had creative differences."

Eddie suspected financial differences. He suspected Sanderson wouldn't go for Sam's super-lowball rate. "Well ... you've got a much better director in me," Eddie said with forced confidence. "Tell me about the script."

"Sentimental, but not entirely a weepy. It's pretty good, based on a self-published novel. Tami Romans brought it to us. Majestic Channel responded, so here we are."

Mike entered the office and handed Eddie a freshly bound script, the heat of the copy machine still warm on its pages, the chemical scent of toner still fresh. Mike said, "It's got a few good supporting roles, and it's well-structured for act breaks."

Eddie remembered from their last picture that Mike was quick to offer story notes and considered himself a writer even though he'd yet to earn a credit. A budding writer/producer; who knew if Mike could write?

"But," Sam said, "Tami's kind of pissed off it didn't work out with Sanderson."

"But not pissed off enough to walk away," Mike said with sarcasm.

Sam offered, "Tami hasn't worked in a while, and I'm betting she needs the job."

Eddie could relate, asked, "So she's definitely in?"

"This is a labor of love, so she's in, yeah, but that battle-ax is insisting on all her own hair-and-makeup team, plus some stylist. All these bitches are costing me a fortune." Sam tapped his clenched fist to the middle of his chest as if calming progressive heartburn. He grimaced and washed it down with his nearby can of Diet Coke.

"What's our schedule?" Eddie asked.

"As usual, fourteen days," said Sam.

Eddie nodded. He'd worked that schedule before but never on a period piece. He could already see this project was going to be a challenge.

Sam waved his Diet Coke and said, "Read the script, and if you're interested I'll set up a meeting. You may have to warm Tami up, boost her confidence, so to speak. She's got director approval."

With Tami having a final say, Eddie began to wonder how he would be able to close the deal. What if she didn't like him? Who would Sam move on to next?

"Is the network happy with just Tami?" Eddie asked. "Or are there more names involved?"

"We'll wedge in a few familiar character actors, but we don't have the budget for any more bankable names, per se. Network's fine with that. Tami has a few ideas. Maybe you do too. Talk to her about it."

"When does it start?"

"Saturday. I had Stuart Hardwicke make the schedule, you remember Stuart. He'll be your first."

Eddie did remember Stuart, Sam's go-to first assistant director. Although Eddie had engaged in heated arguments with Stuart when their last project fell behind schedule, by the end of the week they'd caught up and the TV movie came in under budget. Eddie figured

Stuart was a solid choice, but he was a shouter and had an ego. Eddie hated how Stuart could be pompous and boisterous to the cast and crew. If it were Eddie's choice, he would have hired someone else, someone more chill and confident, but he knew Sam felt secure with an AD from his own camp. He also suspected he chose Stuart to keep him informed of everything in his absence. Eddie thought Sam could be the poster boy for attention deficit disorder. Executive Producer Sam didn't have the patience to be on set for more than a few hours a day, so Stuart would be his eyes and ears.

"Where are we shooting?" Eddie asked.

"Crescent Movie Ranch, up in the mountains, way up off Angeles Crest Highway." Sam got up from his chair. "There's a Western town set, a ranch house and barn, a small pond and a schoolhouse. Disney just shot part of a feature up there. They've added on to the existing sets, painted it all and created a few new practical interiors, so the place looks great. We'll be the first to exploit it. I had the screenwriter go up there last week and adapt the script to what's already in place. Art department's moving props up tomorrow, I think." Sam shot a look to Mike who confirmed with a nod. "A lot of our crew is already set and ready to go."

"Sounds good," Eddie replied.

"If you choose to do it," Sam continued, "I'd like to use Giovanni to lens this thing since you two have worked together."

"Giovanni's great," Eddie said. Giovanni was a fast and effective cinematographer and it was becoming more and more obvious that Sam was keeping this one in the family. Eddie also knew that Giovanni had worked with Chris Sanderson in the past so he figured the cinematographer was hired before Sanderson dropped out.

"Tami has approval of the cameraman as well," said Sam, "but Giovanni knows what the hell he's doing. Besides, he's got plenty of gauze in his kit."

Mike burst out laughing.

It took a second for Eddie to understand the joke. Sam was

referring to the old-school Hollywood practice of placing a thin layer of medical gauze behind the lens to soften wrinkles when photographing aging actresses.

Mike piped in with, "We haven't accounted for the camera department charging an extra kit rental on all that gauze. I'll add a line item to the budget."

Laughs around the room, this time Eddie joining in.

"Tell you what," Eddie offered, "Since time is of the essence, I'll read the script in your conference room. We can talk after. That work?"

"Great," Sam said. "If it's for you, I'll set up a meeting with Tami tomorrow morning."

Without even reading the script Eddie knew he'd take the job.

—

CHAPTER THREE

Sheila couldn't get the image out of her mind, her mother's transition across the threshold of death.

Her mom's face had turned a shade of purple, then slightly green, orange, and then finally an ashen yellow. Like colors of the rainbow. Since the pillowcase in the hospital was yellow Sheila wondered if the final phase of dying had something to do with it. Maybe, like a chameleon, nature finds a way to blend its dead into the surroundings.

Now Sheila was alone.

Sitting in the SuperShuttle van in tangled LAX traffic, that image played over and over in Sheila's mind. And then, the moment after her mother passed away, there was the strange feeling that someone was standing over her shoulder. Sheila turned but nobody was there. Later, drinking alone, she came to the conclusion it must have been the angel of death as she wrestled with both guilt and sadness. Or maybe it was just the angel to take her mom to heaven. Something was there. She was certain.

A cheap ballpoint pen had been the murder weapon.

Since Sheila was an only child, she had to be the one to sign the official form that allowed the hospital team to take her mother off life support.

A stroke of a pen.

Sheila stole that ballpoint pen. The next morning, as if it were a spent revolver reeking of gunpowder, she threw the evidence into Taggart Creek. She wanted it to sink but it didn't. The pen floated to the bank. *Shit.*

After her mother had passed, Sheila spent the following week dealing with the funeral arrangements and cleaning out the townhome. There was so much stuff to go through, a lifetime's worth of memories, family photos, furniture. She arranged a self-storage unit because she was not ready to let the stuff go. Not yet, anyway. She needed more time.

Only twenty-seven years old, Sheila felt old. Now she would have nowhere to go when Christmas came around—no mom to call on Sunday or send flowers to on Mother's Day.

She never knew her father. He'd gone back to Australia before she was born. She had no relationship with him whatsoever, so there would be no dad to walk her down the aisle if and when her wedding day ever came. Not that her mother, in a motorized wheelchair, could have done that anyway.

It was an early flight out of Raleigh, North Carolina, so she didn't get a chance to call her boyfriend, Roland. Other than a few texts, it had been over two days since they'd talked. Sheila missed him. She hadn't seen him in well over three weeks, not since the day her mother was moved from the assisted living facility to the hospital, the same day Sheila flew back home. That seemed like so long ago.

All she wanted was a hot shower and to hold Roland and cry.

She was about to call him when her phone rang instead: Giovanni. Work, maybe. She answered with as much cheerfulness as she could muster.

"Hey, Giovanni."

"Sheila, how are you, darling?"

"Oh, I'm, a … doin' all right."

"You don't sound so."

"I just got back into town."

"Where have you been?"

"Oh …" She didn't have a lie ready so decided to just tell him the truth. "My mother passed away and I had to deal with everything."

"Oh, I'm sorry, my dear. I'll call back later," he said.

"No, no … it's good to hear from you. Don't hang up."

"It's nothing important. It's just …"

"Giovanni, I'm fine, and glad you called. What's on your mind?"

"How you say?" English was not his first language and he searched for the way to phrase it. "Just putting the word out, darling, I believe that's the expression, no? There's a film starting up next week, TV movie, I'm afraid, but such is life."

Sheila had first worked with Giovanni years ago when he was relatively new to Los Angeles. She realized he had complete control of the English language but also knew him well enough to recognize a pattern—pour on the accent when a dash of continental charm worked in his favor. It seemed over the years, his accent was becoming more and more prominent, not less so.

"The project is out of town," Giovanni continued, "up in the mountains, but for only two weeks. Not a lot of money, but … I don't have the job yet myself, it's complicated and nobody is committing … so stupid, but if it's meant to be, are you available, my dear?"

Sheila was proud to be Giovanni's first choice as his assistant cameraperson. She had learned so much from him over the years. Sure, he could be unreasonable and fly off the handle at times, but she really enjoyed working for him. He had a great aesthetic eye and treated his crew with respect. He made the work fun.

Giovanni also encouraged Sheila to break out on her own and become a cinematographer in her own right. This was not an easy task since the profession was predominantly male, but this was her dream, to create art and great drama with the camera. She'd make it happen. She'd *will* it.

Over the years, Sheila had built a reputation for mastering the first assistant cameraperson's most important skill: keeping the subject in focus. Since Giovanni preferred to use long lenses, and move the camera as much as possible, the task of keeping focus demanded a Zen-like concentration. Rarely, if ever, did she blow a shot. Sheila rose to the challenge.

"Yeah, Giovanni, I'm available," she said, even though she could have used a long rest to sleep off the burden of grief and sadness. But on the other hand, she thought maybe getting out of town and immersing herself in work might just be the perfect remedy. "I'm your girl," she said.

"And for that," Giovanni replied, "I am grateful."

"Who's directing?"

"Chris Sanderson."

Sheila remembered working with Chris Sanderson once before, a perpetually tanned, energetic old-school director with decades of experience under his belt.

"Sounds good. When do I prep the camera package?"

"As soon as Friday. I'll get back to you once I know more. I am sorry to hear about your mother. Is there is anything I can do?"

"No, but thank you. Work is good. It's what I need right now."

"You sure?"

"Yes."

"Arrivederci."

"Ciao," she said and hung up.

She worried about breaking the news to Roland. Having been gone for almost a month now, she'd be back for only a few days and then possibly gone for *another* couple of weeks. Maybe he could drive up to the mountains and join her. He did that once, came to location for a couple of days when they first started dating. That was a good memory.

Next, she called Roland but only got his voice mail. New passengers were getting onto the van so she did not feel comfortable leaving a message. She would call him when she got home.

The shuttle weaved onto Sepulveda Boulevard. It passed an In-N-Out Burger and she caught the scent of fried onions. The smell was strangely comforting. It felt good to be home.

The shuttle dropped Sheila off in front of her Santa Monica apartment. She tipped the driver and picked up her bags, stepping over the dried palms that had been blown down from the trees that lined her block. She could hear a steady wind rustling the palms above.

At her door, digging into her luggage for the key, a premonition hit. Something felt off. Was her roommate, Lisa, home? Was everything okay? Turning the lock, she could hear Lisa's muffled voice coming from her bedroom.

Then she heard Roland's laugh.

Are they going to surprise me?

A yelp—but not one of distress. That was clearly pleasure.

Fearing the worst, Sheila moved to the hallway, only to see Roland and Lisa going at it, tangled in the black satin sheets.

Sheila's heart dropped. Betrayal—both of them.

How could they?

She turned and headed out the door.

"Sheila?" Lisa called out, then added a muffled, "Oh, Christ."

Sheila grabbed her bags and ran out. Outside the apartment she saw Roland's Mercedes parked on the street. *How did I miss that? Shit!*

She marched into the underground parking garage lugging her heavy bags. She tossed them into her Toyota, started her car, and screeched up the concrete ramp.

Sheila had to get out of there.

CHAPTER
FOUR

San Bernardino County Deputy Sheriff Sondra Martinez had unearthed plenty of bodies before. The vast majority had been discovered in shallow graves or dumped off rocky cliffs. This was a first; murder by arrow.

The mountains and high desert in her jurisdiction had long been a popular dumping ground for gang-related corpses, and ever since the department brought on cadaver dogs, more and more bodies had been found. But this investigation was different. The victim had been murdered while changing his tire after hitting a deer. The victim's face was crushed beyond recognition, and the deer lay near the smashed car. Brain matter from both man and beast was splayed across the pavement.

A motorist had called it in at dawn and Deputy Martinez was the first on the scene. Now the road had been blocked in both directions and more than a dozen of her colleagues assisted in the investigation. The department's helicopter searched from above while Detective Chong delegated the responsibilities. Kenny Chong was the middle-aged veteran who handled the majority of the homicides in San Bernardino County. Since this murder was so brazen, he'd called in the cavalry. The detective worked primarily down in the cities of San Bernardino and Redlands. Over the years he'd never given Deputy Martinez the time of day.

Martinez waited until he was done meeting with the crime scene techs before she approached. "Got a second?" she asked.

He gave her a nod.

"I was thinking," she said, "these arrows ... not all that common."

"What's on your mind?" he said, not really looking at her, scanning the surroundings over her head. Detective Chong was over six feet tall, whereas Deputy Martinez was short in stature, under five feet. Although there was no official minimum height requirement in the sheriff's department, she'd spent her entire career battling the handicap. To make light of it she'd often joked with her colleagues that she was "vertically challenged even in heels."

Martinez said, "I know a pair of brothers up here, the Dillards. Their mom died a couple years back, left them the place. I suspect they're bowhunters."

"You've seen them out hunting?" he asked.

"No," she recalled, "but there was an alpaca shot."

"Excuse me?"

"An alpaca, which is basically a miniature llama," she explained. "People get the things as pets. Some fleece them for their wool to weave sweaters or satchels."

"I'm familiar with alpacas. When did this happen?"

"Last year. Couldn't connect the Dillard brothers, but the neighbor who owned the animal was certain they did it. I went out to their place and saw targets they'd set up, sheepskin rugs draped over hay bales and dummies tied to trees all with arrows stuck in them. They denied they'd shot the animal even though one of them admitted the alpaca spit on him."

"Spit?"

"Alpacas are like camels. They chew their cud and are known to spit without any provocation, up to twenty-five feet away," she said, having learned this fact during the investigation.

"Revenge killing?"

"Possible motive. I have no idea why either of them would have reason to kill this guy while he was changing his tire, but with the arrows and all …"

"Will they remember you?"

"Yes."

"Lieutenant DeLuca," Chong called out.

The lieutenant approached with, "Sir."

"I need you to draft some of your men and accompany Deputy Martinez to question a pair of local bowhunters," he said.

"Ten-four," DeLuca said and shot a familiar look to Sondra. They knew each other from years ago when they both worked the jails. As is the case with Los Angeles County Sheriff's Department recruits, they'd started their careers assigned to jail duty. She'd learned a lot about career criminals and remembered how DeLuca showed little fear when engaging the worst of the inmates. Rugged and smart, he'd gained respect from both colleagues and the hardened prisoners who knew not to test him.

Once their jail duty was fulfilled, she and DeLuca went their separate ways. Whereas she was assigned to the San Bernardino National Forest, he'd worked the drug-ridden cities in the valley below. He'd even assisted in the gun battle connected to the San Bernardino terrorist attack years ago. Sondra figured that was why he'd been promoted to lieutenant.

"Where we going, Martinez?" he asked.

"Keller Peak Road," she said.

"We'll take my car."

Another sheriff's vehicle followed while Martinez rode shotgun in DeLuca's cruiser. She could see his was the newest model with tech upgrades. Sondra's car was considerably older, having once served in the pool of vehicles to transfer prisoners. Its back-seat steel partition rattled, which annoyed her. No vibration in this car—DeLuca's felt tight and ran smooth.

After she brought him up to speed about the alpaca incident, the car fell silent until he mentioned his wife had just given birth to their second girl. This prompted Martinez to talk about her son.

"Cesar's my little boy's name."

"How old?"

"Five. Already a Dodger fan."

"His dad must be proud."

"He is," she said, not going into the fact that she wasn't married to the father of her child. Family life had scared Lewis off, and technically they never married. What broke her heart was that Lewis rarely visited his son. He sent a few hundred dollars a month for child support, but that barely covered the childcare expense when she was off at work. Talk of Cesar reminded her to text Mrs. Gomez, the sitter, and let her know she'd be late.

By the time Martinez got to the hospital, the day Cesar was born, his head was already crowning and it was too late to administer an epidural. The baby was in an awkward position and the pain giving birth was so overwhelming she thought she was going to die. But she found strength within. She remembered the expression of the doctor's face afterward, amazed, as if she'd just lifted a car. God's gift for surviving that day was a baby boy that changed her life forever. She'd read that because of childbirth, women have a significantly higher tolerance for pain than their male counterparts. Martinez believed it.

"Must be nice," DeLuca said, "working up here in the mountains."

"Has its pluses and minuses. I deal with a lot of tourists."

"Not many tourists in my beloved San Bernardino," he said dryly.

She laughed, knowing San Bernardino laid claim to being one of California's ten worst places to live. Not a tourist destination, and never would be. Sondra said, "It's hard to follow up. Something happens to a tourist," she said, "they just want to go home."

"Isn't that true for all of us?"

"What's that?"

"That we all just want to go home."

"True," she said. She wondered what Mrs. Gomez, the old lady who watched over a handful of children in her apartment complex, would make Cesar for dinner tonight. Hopefully something healthy this time.

They came across the dirt road that led to the Dillard place. There was nothing but a dilapidated mailbox and a pair of tire tracks leading into the mountain property. "You can't see the house from the road," she said. "Probably best to park on the shoulder and walk in."

"What makes you think they're home?" he asked.

"Gut feeling," she said. Sondra couldn't explain it much more beyond that.

DeLuca pulled over and crept to a stop. Officers Simmons and Lutz pulled up behind. Simmons was an African American, and Lutz was his wiry partner, both in their late twenties. They spread out and marched into the property.

The first thing Martinez noticed was all the trash splayed everywhere, much of it caught in the dried weeds, discarded candy wrappers and Big Gulp soft drink cups. There was none of this the last time she'd been on the property. Wildlife had been known to get into trash receptacles and spread refuse, but this felt different. It was as if the Dillard brothers had stopped using their trash can and the evidence at her feet suggested they lived on a diet of sugary junk food.

Through the trees she could see the unkempt Victorian house and a shiny SUV. What was also different from the last time she'd been there was the double-wide trailer next to the home. It was brand new. She didn't see any of the impromptu archery targets from last time. Things felt different.

A dog began barking from inside the house.

DeLuca halted and motioned the others to do the same. "Smell that?" he said.

"What?" asked Simmons.

"That odor."

Sondra caught the scent he was referring to. "Cat piss?" she said.

"Ammonia. Could be a meth lab," DeLuca said.

She'd suspected the brothers were heavy partyers but never imagined they'd be manufacturing methamphetamine. "All these candy wrappers," Sondra said, pointing to the trash in the weeds, "the diet of tweakers."

"What do we do, chief?" Simmons asked.

"Come back another day with our friends from the DEA," Lieutenant DeLuca said. He gave the double-wide one last look then turned back.

The gunshot startled Martinez.

The tree beside her took the bullet's impact.

Chips of bark exploded into her eyes. Sondra instinctively dropped down and pulled her Glock—couldn't see a thing.

Another gunshot. It came from the house. Simmons, Lutz, and DeLuca fired back.

She caught sight of the toolshed they were firing upon a moment before Jerry Dillard made a break for it. Before she could raise her weapon, Jerry was hit. His legs spun out from under him. More shots rang out, the guys still firing for good measure. Face planted in the dirt, Jerry Dillard twitched as dirt kicked up all around him.

Simmons ran up while DeLuca and Lutz trained their weapons on the house. Simmons tossed Jerry's rifle aside, drove a knee into his vertebrae, and handcuffed him as he squirmed facedown in the dirt.

Her ears ringing, Martinez trained her gun at the double-wide trailer and said, "His brother must be close."

DeLuca called it in.

CHAPTER FIVE

Eddie had to run a few errands before returning to his Venice Beach apartment. First, he dropped by Vidiots, an eclectic video rental store that carried DVD back-titles. The shop had almost gone out of business years ago until some anonymous Good Samaritan infused cash to save the establishment. All of the independent bookstores Eddie used to frequent were long gone so he was grateful a place like Vidiots was still in business. He figured he could dig up a couple of Tami Romans titles there.

"Tami Romans, I remember her," the young, tattooed clerk wearing a chain-mail shirt said. "My mom used to watch her show *Guiding Spirit.*"

"What do you think of her?" Eddie asked the guy, testing.

"No opinion, but I don't have cable, bro. I watch YouTube and Japanese animé mostly. But I guess she's all right for TV and shit."

Exactly, Eddie thought. This guy was certainly not the audience for a movie on the Majestic Channel. Eddie was well aware of the trend, a younger generation that doesn't subscribe to cable, fleeing conventional television like rats from a sinking ship. That's why, he knew, decent cable license fees had been diminishing so much from year to year. In the back of his mind, Eddie wondered if he should change professions, the trend of entertainment tastes sliding away from television.

But what would I do? What marketable skills do I have?

On the other hand, he knew people had an insatiable thirst for content. Viewers may not be sitting on their couch watching cable TV as often, but Majestic's audience wasn't part of that younger demographic. They wouldn't be viewing movies on their cell phones with earbuds on.

He trusted there was still an audience—still a need. He searched the shelves and found a handful of DVDs featuring Tami in a variety of roles.

Next, he needed to pick up a new shirt to wear to tomorrow's breakfast. He had not done laundry in two weeks so a fresh shirt was critical. The breakfast meeting was scheduled at Shutters, a trendy beach-chic hotel a mile or so from his one-bedroom apartment. He knew the tab there would be pricey. Eddie hoped that if he didn't get the job he could expense the meal to Carver Entertainment and, hopefully, they'd process it quickly before the mailman brought his credit card statement.

On the sale rack in Santa Monica's Banana Republic on the Third Street Promenade he found a hip-looking Western-styled button-down, a Western shirt for a Western. *Perfect.*

Lastly, he hit the market for a frozen pizza and a six-pack of beer. Since he didn't have the job yet, Eddie decided not to splurge. The pizza was on sale and his regular Coors Light was just fine. His plan for the evening was to sit down and go through the script to make notes and watch the Tami movies.

His initial feeling was the script was not bad for a first-time writer, but it was, by no means, great. Schoolteacher from back East, Tami's role, arrives at a remote mining town circa 1880. She turns a rundown barn into a schoolhouse then encourages the children of immigrant miners all working for the mining company to attend. Many of the immigrant families rely on the slave wages the children earn performing their menial jobs. Tami's character has to make her case and there are a few righteous monologues touting the importance of education. There's a little romance too, a love triangle. The wealthy outfitter comes courting, but it's the talented and sensitive blacksmith with a mysterious past who (we discover in the middle of the second act) deserves her love most. Schmaltzy sure, but, *What the hell?* Eddie figured it might broaden his horizons.

Returning home, he needed a clean environment before he could concentrate. The apartment was hot so he opened windows and went about tossing old *Daily Racing Forms* and vacuuming potato chips off the carpet, remnants from a party with his stoner neighbors from two nights before. He discovered a container of onion dip under the couch, crusty and discolored. Eddie didn't remember that item from the other night and wondered how long it had been there.

Next, he cleaned out the refrigerator, tossing out long-forgotten takeout containers and packets of ketchup and soy sauce.

Later, after reading the script again, he fast-forwarded through the different movies he'd rented only watching the scenes with Tami and checked out some of her old TV series available on Netflix. It was clear Tami's strength was drama, her long-burning reactions and doe-like eyes—always with vulnerability woven into her stoic performance. There was a dreadful romantic comedy from early in her career in which Tami felt miscast. Her comic timing was off.

Most of the frozen pizza and three beers in, he noticed a peculiar trend. In almost every scene, Tami was on the left side of screen with the camera featuring the right side of her face. Going back through the DVDs, it didn't appear to be a coincidence.

She has a good side.

Eddie noted this detail in his script and wondered if Tami

would feel embarrassed if he mentioned it. *Do I bring this up? Will it help me get the job?*

Bored with the DVDs, he got on the internet to view the Santa Anita race replays. Examining the results, it was probably a good thing he didn't spend the day at the track because most of his picks didn't hit the board. Rough estimation—he probably saved fifty or sixty dollars by not placing those bets.

Maybe my luck is turning around.

Work done for the day, he thought about hitting one of the late-night bars to try to meet girls but he was too broke and didn't feel like taking a shower and shaving. It was times like this that he felt most lonely—tasks finished for the day and nobody to share his thoughts with.

Someday.

Sitting alone in his apartment, battling his usual loneliness and depression, Eddie finished the last of his beers.

CHAPTER
SIX

Deputy Sheriff Sondra Martinez hovered over a bleeding Jerry Dillard.

The sheriffs had gone through the property and there was no sign of Nick, Jerry's younger brother, so Sondra interrogated Jerry for his whereabouts. Jerry refused to answer, cursing through clenched teeth before he passed out. She stayed back in the trees until the rest of the team arrived, followed by agents from the DEA. The paramedics attended to the unconscious Jerry before they hauled him away.

The team broke the heavy lock and entered the double-wide trailer. Sondra followed them in and could see it was clearly a meth lab—heavy ammonia smell, blackened windows, plastic tubs of chemicals. There was an industrial oven with propane tanks below a makeshift ventilation system.

She noted there was nothing mounted on the bare paneled walls other than a velvet painting of Elvis. Martinez hadn't seen a Velvet Elvis in a long time. A spotlight clamped to the ceiling illuminated the painting as if it were a Rembrandt hanging in a museum. Elvis held the microphone with a stream of tears dripping from one eye. She remembered these souvenirs sold alongside faux sheepskin upholstery covers on gas station corners and hawked by roaming Tijuana vendors to tourists waiting in the long lines in their cars to return to the United States. As a child she'd waited in that line countless times with her family after they'd visited her grandma and cousins over Easter. She'd gazed in wonder at the dayglow velvet paintings of Elvis, Lucha Libre masked wrestlers, and Our Lady of Guadalupe. She remembered the unbearable heat and the smell of exhaust that gave her headaches as a child.

"I've always wondered," she said to DeLuca, "in all these Velvet Elvis paintings, why is he crying? What makes Elvis so sad?"

"Something to do with Priscilla?" DeLuca proposed, deadpan.

"More likely his mom," Officer Simmons informed them.

"Why's that?" asked Martinez.

"It's common knowledge that Elvis was a momma's boy," Simmons said matter-of-factly.

"Copy that," DeLuca affirmed, then added dryly, "a bona fide Memphis momma's boy."

"Just the facts," Simmons returned with a nod.

Martinez could see the guys had the old-school, Jack Webb / Sergeant Friday routine down. "In jailhouse tattoos," Sondra remembered from her days working the jails, "isn't a tear the symbol of murder ... the mourning of a tragic death?"

"That's right," DeLuca said, "for both cholos and the white supremacists."

Martinez noted, "It's the only thing on the walls in here, Elvis crying ... could it have some kind of significance?"

"Meaning what?" asked DeLuca.

Martinez didn't have an answer. "I don't know."

Having overheard them, Detective Chong piped in. "Velvet paintings were made popular by painter Edgar Leeteg, an American artist living in Tahiti back in the forties and fifties."

There was a pause as all turned to look at Detective Chong. He gave them an affirmative nod.

"Tahiti?" Martinez said. "I've always thought these things came from Mexico."

This engagement only encouraged Detective Chong, who continued as if he was a professor lecturing to students. "Maybe these days that's the case, but it started with Leeteg. He painted naked Polynesian women and was known as the American Gauguin. My dad had one of Leeteg's paintings, but my mom was so embarrassed by it she made him take it down. At first only before guests came over, but then permanently. As a kid, I was fascinated by the thing. Dad claimed it was worth a lot of money."

"A velvet painting?" asked DeLuca.

"That's right. A Leeteg."

"I doubt this Velvet Elvis is worth very much, sir," DeLuca said. Simmons stifled a laugh.

Detective Chong turned to the crime scene photographer and said, "Get a shot of the King."

The tech snapped away.

After they'd coaxed the German shepherd out of the house, the team cleared the home. Like the trailer, the house was new territory for Sondra. The last time she was on the Dillard property, she'd interviewed the brothers on the porch and hadn't entered.

Martinez was appalled at how disgusting the place was. Clutter was everywhere, yellowed newspapers stacked high. These Dillard brothers were clearly hoarders.

There was a pair of sweat-stained velour La-Z-Boy recliners in front of a giant TV. She pointed out the dog feces on the floor so others wouldn't step in it.

"In here," Lieutenant DeLuca said.

The walls were decorated by a Confederate flag and assorted Elvis memorabilia, and multiple rifles and shotguns leaned against the walls. This downstairs bedroom appeared to be their arsenal. Sondra noticed a black hunting bow slung over a cracked vinyl chair.

"This could be our smoking gun," she said, pointing it out to Detective Chong.

"Good work, Martinez," he said.

Making sure not to touch anything, she examined the accessories aside the bow, which included a quiver filled with brass-tipped arrows. These arrowheads appeared different than the ones collected at the roadside. Whereas the arrowheads at the crime scene had multiple beveled blades, these were simply sharpened metallic tips. Sondra noticed something else before she said aloud, "There are two of everything here, arm guards, archery gloves ... but something's missing."

"What?" asked Detective Chong.

"The other bow."

CHAPTER
SEVEN

Eddie left early so he could find a parking spot on the street. This was not an easy task so close to the beach, but avoiding the hotel's valet service was his plan. There was the possibility his breakfast meeting with Tami would conclude outside Shutters Hotel as they waited for their vehicles. He didn't want her to judge him once the valet guy delivered his beat-up Subaru. Plus, it was yet another expense, another outlay of cash—not to mention the tip. If he didn't get the job, the fewer receipts he had to submit to Sam Carver the better.

Eddie entered the hotel lobby and rounded a massive floral arrangement. He moved past an array of plush white couches and descended the stairs leading to the beach-level restaurant.

Scanning the tables, he did not see her, so he let the staff know he was expecting someone. The hostess, a petite Asian girl, seated him.

He was ordering coffee just as Tami arrived. He waved, stood, and they greeted each other beside the table.

His first impression was that she appeared older than he'd

expected. He figured probably late fifties or early sixties. *Who could tell?* Tami was smaller than he'd imagined. Her shoulder-length hair hung loose, a salon-enhanced reddish-blond that appeared to have been curled at the ends. Her pale skin had the look of expensive professional treatments and he was pretty sure she'd had some work done. She wore a flowing hippie-styled beach dress, casual yet pricey-looking, and craft jewelry. Eddie was familiar with the look, a cross between flower-child Topanga Canyon and beach-chic Malibu.

"Nice to meet you," he said.

"Likewise," was her cheerful response, taking his hand and clasping it with both of hers. The overeager waiter pulled out her chair with a saccharine smile. Tami thanked him and said, "I'll have green tea, please."

After they were seated, Eddie reminded himself he needed to place the cloth napkin in his lap, table etiquette. He needed to make a good impression.

"Sam tells me you're a very talented director," she said.

"That's nice of him to say that. I think we work well together," Eddie replied, trying to keep things bright and positive. "It really boils down to the art of collaboration, what I do … what *we* do, working as a team," he said, trying to communicate he would be open to her ideas, or at least willing to listen.

Before she could respond, the flamboyant waiter was back with menus, "Good morning," he said with forced enthusiasm. "And how are *we* doing this morning?" He obviously recognized Tami.

His overzealousness annoyed Eddie.

"Good morning," Tami said. "Fine, thank you."

He informed them about the special, lobster eggs Benedict, and after more irksome pleasantries, he spun on his heels and was off.

Eddie hated the guy.

"I'm sorry, but I must admit," Tami said, "I'm not familiar with your work."

"Ah ... the scourge of so many of us indie filmmakers," he half-joked.

"Sam was kind enough to rush over a Blu-ray of your last film, but I haven't had a chance to see it."

"We were challenged by a short schedule," Eddie said. "But we had a really good cast and I'm proud of that little movie." In truth, it wasn't a little movie for him at all. It had a far bigger budget than most of Eddie's endeavors.

Tami said, "Sam insisted we meet, which I am more than happy to do, but as you must know Chris Sanderson is in negotiations to direct."

What the fuck? Am I even in the running for this job? Is this just a courtesy meeting? Eddie nodded, considered what she'd just said, wondering, *Is she testing me?*

"Chris is solid," he said with the best poker face he could muster, "and you'll be in good hands, but Sam suggested we meet in the event Chris Sanderson is not available. Sam mentioned something about a scheduling conflict?"

"Yes," she said. "I'm confident Sam can move our schedule around to accommodate, but just in case ..."

Eddie nodded silently. He noticed she appeared more relaxed now that the air was clear. He considered excusing himself to call Sam Carver from the men's room. *What the fuck, Sam? Is Sanderson still on this thing or what?*

"So, tell me about yourself," she said.

Eddie sipped his coffee before he started in. He told her about how he'd grown up in San Diego, attended film school at USC, and then worked at a New York ad agency. Tami countered with her own story, her childhood in Connecticut, her drama training at Yale. She dropped Yale a few times, he noted. She told him about her work as an animal-rights activist and the foundation she'd created to care for abused animals and abandoned pets.

The waiter returned. "Have you had a chance to decide?" he asked Tami.

"Oh, why, yes," then to Eddie, Tami asked, "and you?"

Eddie gave her a nod. "I think so." He could see the waiter hadn't taken his eyes off Tami, hanging on every word as she ordered the seasonal fruit plate and a mimosa.

Eddie was relieved that she felt at ease enough to have a drink. This opened the door for him to have an adult beverage. He could certainly go for one, especially with all this talk of Chris Sanderson. He decided on the cinnamon French toast accompanied by a Bloody Mary, but held his tongue to make it a double.

"Ex … cellent choice," the waiter said, drawing it out, nodding and jotting on his little pad. "We'll get right on that," he said to Tami, spun around again, and was off.

Give it a break, Eddie thought.

Glowing, Tami watched him go.

Eddie could see she liked to be pampered. He sipped his coffee again and said, "I had an American history teacher in high school who claimed it wasn't the men who settled the West, but rather the women." He could see he'd piqued her interest. "Sure, the men herded cattle, plowed fields, built fences, had gunfights in the streets, and all, but it was the women who raised the families and brought culture and civilization to the frontier. They deserve the real credit but were never written about in the newspapers and periodicals of the time. When I read the script, I couldn't help but remember that. I thought about your character bringing education and integrity to the little mining community, settling the West, but not on a dusty street … rather at a dusty chalkboard."

Her eyes lit up.

Where he came up with the *dusty chalkboard* metaphor he'd never know. Sometimes Eddie surprised himself.

She said, "You should meet Fran, who wrote the script based on her wonderful novel."

"I'd like to."

Their drinks arrived, and Eddie could tell his was watered down. *Bastards.*

They spoke about the characters. When Tami asked what he thought of the script, Eddie was honest. He told her he felt the bad guy, in this case the town's dry-goods merchant, was not bad enough. He offered a few suggestions to make him more hateable. His thoughts included expanding a scene where Bartholomew demonstrates intolerance dealing with the town's dirt-poor Native Americans.

"I thought Tom Birch would be good in that role," Tami said.

"He's good. I can certainly see him very likable up front when he's introduced and begins to court you, but then he turns unpredictable. Tom has that quality, to be both charming and a little scary … even at the same time."

"Sounds like my ex-husband," Tami said.

They shared a laugh.

She said, "I worked with Tom when he was a recurring character on my series and he's quite good. We've remained friends over the years."

"He's a good choice," Eddie said, and could see the wheels turning in her head. He wondered what she was thinking. Their conversation moved on to recent movies and TV shows.

The waiter returned and gave his final saccharine spiel before dropping off the check. Tami was quick to grab it. She already had her credit card out and waved the waiter back.

"No, Tami, this one's on me," Eddie said, reaching for the binder.

"Nonsense," Tami said pulling it away. "My treat."

He didn't know if this was a good or a bad sign. Eddie figured it was probably bad. Tami agreed to meet with Sam's director so she'll most likely expense the receipt as proof. Eddie Lyons gets his hopes up, a free breakfast, and a weak Bloody Mary, but Chris Sanderson gets the job.

Story of my life.

As Eddie predicted, they bid goodbye outside the hotel waiting for Tami's car. Since he did not have a valet ticket Eddie felt the need to explain that he lived close enough to walk. Then, figuring he had nothing to lose, he asked, "I've seen a lot of your movies and have a technical question, if you don't mind me asking."

"Yes?" she said with an air of caution.

"I sense you prefer stage right. Am I right?"

"What do you mean by that?"

"It's only because I'm in the business, but I've noticed a pattern. I get the feeling most of your scenes are blocked in a way that you're on the left side of screen, especially the scenes in profile. Is that a conscious decision, or just coincidence?" Eddie asked. He could see he'd struck a nerve.

"I hadn't thought about it," she said, but he could tell she was lying.

Just then her sleek Tesla arrived. *Electric car*, he thought. *Another statement.*

"I only ask because I've accommodated actors who prefer one side over the other. Not a problem. Like I said, it's about collaboration, and if it's meant to be I'll do everything in my power to make you look great," Eddie said, lightly touching her arm. "It was nice meeting you."

"Likewise," she said.

"Thank you for breakfast."

He moved on. *That's right, close with the assumption I've already got the job. Confidence.* He could feel her eyes on his back but did not turn back. When he finally did, he could see her white Tesla pull away.

Moments later, on the concrete bike path at the edge of the

sand, Eddie said into the phone, "Sam, there must be some kind of misunderstanding. Tami tells me Chris Sanderson is still directing this thing."

"Bullshit. I told his agent he's out," Sam replied. "They're asking for too much money and there are crazy availability issues."

"That's not what Tami thinks," Eddie said as bicyclists and rollerbladers brushed past.

"What'd she say?"

"She thought she was meeting me out of courtesy."

"I bet Sanderson hasn't told her, that slippery old bastard. Or maybe his agent hasn't told Sanderson it's not going to work. Maybe the agent is hoping I'll reconsider or hire another one of his clients. So, how'd the meeting go?"

"I think we hit it off. You know, she's got a good side."

"A what?"

"I'll explain when I get the job."

"Don't worry. I'll call her agent and let him know. If she signs off on you as our director then Mike will contact you with the production meeting details for tomorrow morning."

"Tomorrow?"

"Eddie, we're shooting in four days, with or without you."

"With Sanderson?"

"Fuck Sanderson!" Sam shouted. "For Chrissake, relax. Go home, read the script again, do your laundry, pack. Put a vacation hold on your mail, whatever you need to do. You've gotta be up to speed first thing tomorrow and ready to travel."

"Thanks, Sam. I'm really psyched for the opportunity. Oh, and another thing, I think she wants Tom Birch to play Bartholomew."

"Who?"

"Bartholomew ... the proprietor of the company store."

"No, I mean who's Tom Birch?"

"You know ... character actor ... plays a lot of bad guys. I bet you can get him for scale," Eddie said, referring to the Screen Actor Guild's minimum rate.

"What do you think?"

"If it makes her comfortable, I'm game."

"All the crap that's making her comfortable is costing me a fucking fortune," Sam said, clearly annoyed. "Anything else?"

"That's about it."

"Once I get Tami's approval, you'll be the first to know."

CHAPTER
EIGHT

Tom Birch lectured to his students that same morning.

"Assuming you're lucky enough to be called back," he said, "remember how important it is to wear the same outfit from your first audition. And keep your hair and look the same. Realize the director and producers saw something in you, a potential to play that character, *their* character—it's not yours yet—and quite possibly your wardrobe had something to do with that."

The Hollywood Academy of Dramatic Arts was located on a commercial stretch of Sunset Boulevard in a building that once housed a film and television postproduction facility. Years ago, the mixing boards and dubbing machines were hauled away and the stages were converted into classrooms. Portraits of popular movie stars adorned the walls, none of whom had ever attended this institution.

Tom caught himself staring at one of his young student's breasts, her shapely cleavage accentuated by a clingy V-neck sweater. He remembered she was the one who wore that unique perfume. He diverted his gaze, thought to himself, *That was too obvious*, and pretended to be contemplating deep thoughts to cover it up. He continued, "The audition process is just as it sounds, a 'process' of elimination. Do not eliminate the power of your first impression. *Do* eliminate any doubt in your mind that you're the best choice for the role."

Tom felt his cell phone vibrate in his pocket, so he decided to wrap up his lesson for the day. A few students had questions afterward, always the same ones, but unfortunately not the big-breasted one. After she sauntered out the door, he dealt with the questions from his students then collected his things and headed back to his faculty office cubicle.

Tom had no problem that the Hollywood Academy of Dramatic Arts was not an accredited institution but rather a business built on shaking down twentysomethings, hordes of naive kids with the dream of making it big in Hollywood. He often marveled at how the front office staff was able to chisel financial aid and low-interest student loans out of the federal government. Somehow they were categorized as a legitimate trade school and the trickle-down of guaranteed student loans and subsidized grants were his bread and butter. Tom realized the chances that any of his students would "make it" were slim to none. Most of these hapless kids would be shackled with heavy debt for years to come. This did not bother Tom. He was an actor. They paid him to teach his craft. Teaching three days a week covered his rent between the increasingly rare jobs working in film and television.

Tom's true love was the theater—his crowning achievement was the extended run of Shakespeare's *Richard III* at the Ensemble Theatre of Cincinnati a couple years ago. That was epic. He'd played the title character to rave reviews. Tom still dreamt of those performances, standing on the boards of that great theatre. *Footlights.*

Sitting in his cramped cubicle, he returned the message from his agent. Sarah had good news, an offer for a film with his friend Tami Romans.

"That's great. Who's directing?" was Tom's first question.

"Eddie Lyons," she said.

"Never heard of him."

"Me neither," she said. "I emailed you the script."

Sarah was at one time his ex-agent's assistant until the guy who represented him went into rehab and didn't return to the business, literally dropping off the face of the earth. Sarah took over his clients and had proven herself through hard work and tenacity. Plus, Tom recalled, she had great legs. Tom had fantasized about her the moment he'd seen her, back when she was still an assistant, in her gray business suit and heels, but realized he could never go there. He'd learned through years in show business that it is best not to mix business with pleasure, especially with people he might need something from someday. Flirting with women who held little power, like his students or those who worked on the fringes such as production assistants, wardrobe girls, stage-hands, extras, bit players, and art department broads—well, that was another story.

"When do I read?" he asked.

"I don't think you're going to have to read."

"Really?"

"Tami recommended you and the director knows your work. It looks like you're set if we agree to the terms."

Knows my work? That made Tom feel good. And to not have to audition, that's what separates stars from day-players—to not have to suffer through the tedious audition process he was lecturing about only moments ago.

"They've sent a deal memo, low-budget SAG minimum plus ten, which is all they'll offer. I asked for a pop-out but they won't allow it. They agreed to a two-hold."

From his experience working on location, Tom had been in plenty of two-holds, some of them good, and some not-so-much. Two-hold was industry-speak for individual dressing rooms side by side on a single trailer. Each had its own restroom, which was good, but he knew Tami would get a pop-out star trailer, a full-sized comfort camper with retractable bay windows.

"I can try to negotiate for more," she continued, "but Sam Carver's producing and everyone in town says he's as cheap as they come. I can't guarantee—"

"Do whatever you can, Sarah, and count me in. Tami's a dear friend, as you know, and I'd be thrilled to work with her again. What's the part?"

"Character's name is Bartholomew, the bad guy. I'll email you the synopsis from Breakdown Services."

"Bad guy? No big surprise there," Tom said.

"I remember you saying the bad guys are always the best roles."

"If the part's written well."

"I'm sure you'll be fabulous. If you're available for a fitting today, wardrobe can see you this afternoon. But only *after* I close the deal."

"Of course."

Tom next arranged for a substitute to cover his classes. He downloaded the script and scanned the scenes that included his character. He liked the fact that in most of them, he played against Tami, the star.

His next call was to Tami to thank her and discuss the part. He got her voice mail, so he left a brief message, "So thrilled to be working with you again."

To not have to audition—Tom felt ten feet tall.

CHAPTER
NINE

Eddie's weak Bloody Mary at Tami's courtesy brunch had only lit the pilot light. Back in his apartment, Eddie kept the flame going with a couple of beers and—*What the hell?*—he scraped his pot pipe before smoking the sticky black resin. Sure, it tasted like shit and made him cough, but it chilled him out as he waited for Sam's call.

To keep himself busy, he packed a few pairs of jeans in a duffel bag and made technical notes on the script. Then he started to rough-in a basic shot list he knew Stuart Hardwicke would demand.

He had a solid buzz going and was standing in the bathroom midpee when his phone rang. Without flushing, he buckled his pants and went to the living room to answer.

"Tami was impressed," Sam said, "Congrats, you've got the job."

"Thank you for fighting for me."

"Of course. Let's get to work. I'll have Mike email you the start-up paperwork. Stuart will be calling with details about the schedule."

"Sounds good," Eddie said, wishing now he hadn't toked only

moments ago as talk of assistant director Stuart Hardwicke was definitely a buzzkill. He knew the tedious conversations with Stuart would annoy him, with the guy obsessing over minor details and probably secretly envious *he* wasn't directing.

Sam said, "And call our favorite Italian cameraman, Giovanni, and let him know you guys will be working together. He's already up to speed."

"Sounds good. I'll prep him about Tami and discuss how we can make her look really great." Eddie had some additional ideas about using longer lenses he thought might serve her well. He was curious to hear Giovanni's input.

Sam said, "I'll be honest with you. This picture's going to be a challenge—horses, kids—but you're definitely the man for the job. Keep in mind there's very little contingency built in. We've got to bring this one in on schedule and under budget."

"We did that last time, didn't we?" Eddie reminded Sam.

"That's right, you did. But between you and me, I'm not going to the bank for this one. It's funded by private equity, investors from back East. They're skittish. Do me a favor and just don't go all Federico Fellini on me."

"Fellini?"

"You know what I'm saying. This is not art, Eddie. I need you to direct traffic and stay on schedule."

Eddie laughed and said, "Got it, Sam. We'll keep a tight ship all around."

"I guess I should hang up and call your agent."

"I'm in between representation right now," Eddie said. "My lawyer, Richard, can make my deal." Eddie realized there would be very little negotiation. His rate would be Sam Carver's standard low-budget agreement at Directors Guild minimum, just like last time. Eddie knew the game. The only two guilds represented on the movie would be the Screen Actors Guild because it's impossible to employ name actors like Tami who aren't SAG members, and thankfully the Directors Guild of America because both he and Stuart were members. The budget on this film was low enough so the DGA, under their low-budget agreement, allowed the rates to be negotiable which meant he'd be offered the minimum. No complaints from Eddie. A job was a job.

"You've made my day," Sam said. "One less prick agent I've got to deal with, all the better. Hopefully your lawyer will agree to make this work."

"He will."

"We'll see you at the production meeting."

"Of course, and thanks again," Eddie said before hanging up.

He returned to the bathroom to flush the toilet, watching the amber water swirl around and realizing he really needed to clean the bathroom. Eddie looked at himself in the mirror, thought his eyes looked puffy, and decided he'd better get a haircut.

Another raspy hit from the pot pipe and he was off to Supercuts.

CHAPTER
TEN

Sheila arrived early to the production meeting at Carver Entertainment.

She parked on the street, three blocks away, and hoofed it to the building since she knew the underground garage was off-limits unless you chose to pay for parking. She'd made that mistake on the last movie and had to shell out twelve bucks. *Cheap bastards.* Carver Entertainment would not, under any circumstances, validate. There was no special treatment for below-the-line personnel.

Sheila had spent the last few evenings at her friend Samantha's place and now had a raging headache. Samantha offered her refuge, both a guest room to sleep in and a shoulder to cry on. Not long ago, Samantha had also been betrayed by her boyfriend, so last night they ordered a thin-crust pizza and commiserated over bottles of Trader Joe's Coastal Chardonnay. Samantha was the first friend she'd spoken to since the funeral, so Sheila detailed not only her boyfriend troubles but also the experience of burying her mother.

To talk to someone about it was therapeutic. It felt good to get it off her chest.

Even though Sheila was still tired from jet lag, they stayed up late and she could feel the residual effects from the wine and lack of sleep as she entered the office of Carver Entertainment. Dozens of movie posters decorated the walls, both theatrical B movies from years ago and more recent television titles. In the conference room, a handful of crew were already assembled, none of whom she recognized. She helped herself to a cup of coffee to calm her headache. Portable tables were set up, with foldable chairs surrounding the perimeter. Scripts, call sheets, and schedules on colored paper awaited each participant as if place settings at a dinner party. Sheila was spreading cream cheese on her bagel just as Giovanni arrived. They hugged.

"You all right?"

"Yeah ... thanks for asking," she said. "And thanks again for thinking of me. It couldn't have come at a better time."

"Of course, my darling. We're a team, you and I," he said. "I am so sorry to hear about your mother."

"Thank you."

"If you have second thoughts, or have to bail out for any reason ..." he offered.

"I'll be fine. Like I said, this came at a good time," she said, not ready to tell him about Roland. She so wished Giovanni wasn't gay. *Why can't I find a straight guy like him? Or, at the very least, one who won't sleep with my roommate.* Giovanni's sexual orientation was a well-kept secret. Sheila tried to encourage him come out of the closet, but he told her, for professional reasons, he thought it best not to go public with his personal life.

"Giovanni, you work in show business," she said one night as they drove back from a shoot in Santa Barbara. "Nobody cares."

"The time is not right for me," he said.

She knew him well enough to suspect Giovanni was afraid to admit he was gay to his mother, even though she lived in Palermo, thousands of miles away.

"I'm willing to bet," Sheila said, "she already knows."

"No, no ... she doesn't, I assure you," he insisted.

"Trust me, mothers know everything."

"If she did know she wouldn't try to marry me off to her friends' daughters every time I'm back home."

"She just wants you to be happy," Sheila teased.

"You should see these women. *No man* would be happy."

Giovanni could always make her laugh.

They took a seat just as First Assistant Director Stuart Hardwicke made an entrance and plopped his oversized binder at the head table. Sheila remembered him from the previous Carver Entertainment production.

"Giovanni. Sheila. Good to see you guys again," Stuart said.

"Hey, Stu," she said, chewing her bagel.

"Looks like we've got the band back together, no?" Giovanni said.

"Indeed, my friend. And we're gonna rock," Stuart said, feigning air guitar, trying to make a joke but coming off awkward.

Sheila forced a laugh for his benefit.

Executive Producer Sam Carver entered, flanked by his assistant, Mike. They greeted everyone before sitting at the table alongside Stuart.

Eddie Lyons arrived next. This came as a surprise to Sheila. "I thought Chris Sanderson was directing," she whispered to Giovanni.

"Apparently it didn't work out," he said. "What's the matter?"

"Nothing," Sheila said, hushed. "I'll explain later," just as Eddie sat down next to them.

"Giovanni, my friend," Eddie greeted him with a slap to the cinematographer's back. And then to her he said, "And, hey, Sheila. What's up?"

"Hey Eddie," she said and paged through her paperwork to avoid making eye contact. Eddie took a seat next to Sam Carver and Sheila sunk low into her flimsy foldable chair, avoiding his gaze.

Before she met Roland, at the wrap party of Sam Carver's last film, she had slept with Eddie. She was drunk. He was drunk. Sheila wrote it off as a stupid, tequila-induced mistake.

Eddie was nice enough, but not really her type.

She remembered his hairy back and pale-white gut. The worst part was waking up in his dingy apartment, walls covered in vintage movie posters, and making awkward conversation the morning after. Sheila pretended to be late for a yoga class so she could get out of there and tripped over his Xbox on the way out. She went home to nurse the hangover, regretting it all.

He phoned her that afternoon but she didn't return his call. Eddie continued to leave messages, so she finally called him back and they went out a couple of times, but didn't have sex again. When she realized he wasn't right for her, Sheila broke it to Eddie, told him that she "wasn't in a place to see anyone right now." He seemed disappointed and never called again.

Had she known Eddie was directing this project she would have reconsidered the gig. *More awkward shit to deal with.* Her headache throbbed even worse.

Next, the chief electrician, Paul, entered with the key grip, John, both potbellied guys in their early fifties. Sheila playfully saluted them and they waved back before getting something to eat. Both wore long surfer shorts with industry branded T-shirts. Sheila knew these guys from the last movie. They were a lot of fun, but definitely second-tier crew, or maybe even third, working for the same low wage as she was.

Sheila realized the people in this room, including herself, were not sought-after professionals at the top of their game but rather reliable, workmanlike, below-the-line craftspeople agreeing to Sam Carver's meager, flat day rate. Top dogs worked on theatrical pictures with real budgets and realistic shooting schedules at a semirelaxed pace. Top dogs were hired on movies and TV shows that were shot on comfortable sound stages, with free parking. They earned big bucks in overtime and only needed to work a few projects a year to get by. Between lucrative gigs they enjoyed extended time off and went on vacations with loved ones.

Deep down, Sheila realized the crews working these flat-rate, take-it-or-leave-it indie quickies made up what she referred to as the bottom feeders of the industry.

Bottom feeders.

Sheila didn't want to be a bottom feeder anymore. She aspired to rise to the surface and work on legitimate unionized movies and TV shows that people had actually heard of. But no, instead she was shackled to yet another forgettable television movie her friends would never see, unless they, by chance, stumbled across it on daytime cable.

Bottom feeder. That's me.

The trick, she realized, was to keep working. And rise to the top.

Next, three overaccessorized women entered and sat side by side. One of them had a large black portfolio and propped it up beside her chair. Once settled in, all three pulled sleek aluminum water bottles from their bags and immediately began texting the outside world. Sheila knew the type—*wardrobe, hair, and makeup.*

There were others Sheila did not recognize, a pair of cowboys, a handful of dressed-down types, and as the room filled out, Stuart called the meeting to order.

Sam Carver began and welcomed everyone. He announced how excited he was to be embarking on a project with such a positive message. He suggested they start the meeting with everyone introducing themselves. Sam insisted director Eddie Lyons go first.

Eddie stood and explained how fortunate he was to be back working with Carver Entertainment. "And for those who haven't worked with me before," Eddie said, "feel free to approach with questions, concerns, ideas, wild stories, recipes, what-have-you. This is not *my* movie, but rather *ours.* In the end, it's the sum of all our hard work, blood, sweat, and tears. Well … hopefully not blood, or too many tears, but you get the idea."

Giovanni was next. He stood and proudly said, "I am Giovanni, your devoted director of photography. Since I am Italian, and representing the greatest country in the world, as you all know, I will now freely admit my secret agenda: I vow to make this film a Spaghetti Western." He mimicked drawing guns and firing, held his heart as if shot, then plopped down in his chair. Laughs followed.

A hard act to follow. Sheila briefly introduced herself as the first assistant cameraperson and, with the driest, deadpan delivery she could muster, promised to keep marinara sauce off the lens. More laughs.

Next came John and Paul as key grip and gaffer, tied at the hip, both introducing themselves while still chewing food. The cowboys, named Jimmy and Lucky, were next. By no surprise, they were the animal wranglers. Jimmy spoke about the talented cast of horses whose names included Patches, Misty McCool, and Widowmaker. Before they passed the torch, the assistant wrangler, Lucky, turned to Eddie and said, "I've got snakes and reptiles too if you have need for 'em, sir."

The oldest of the crew, the soft-spoken, gray-haired production designer named Seth, mumbled something about the color palette Sheila didn't entirely understand. To fight boredom, she amused herself with an imaginary backstory for him, that this old hippie had recently escaped from a Santa Fe nudist colony and somehow found his way onto the film.

There were young production assistants, the wiry sound man, a gruff transportation captain with a massive beer gut, and assorted production staff. Two women named Karen and Linda hailed to be the makeup, hair, and wardrobe departments combined.

Finally, the three hipster women introduced themselves as Connie, Miss Roman's "makeup specialist"; Bonnie, Miss Roman's "hair specialist"; and the youngest of the three, Diane, Miss Roman's "stylist." Bonnie and Connie appeared to be in their midforties but were dressed younger in skinny jeans and graphic tees. Diane was in her twenties and the most athletic of the three.

She wore a formfitting sheath dress that Sheila admired.

Stuart explained Tami would have her own makeup trailer and additional staff would be brought in to dress background extras. As they discussed other details, Sheila got the impression Karen and Linda, the other makeup and wardrobe team, were not entirely happy that Tami brought in outside personnel. Sheila predicted there would be much cattiness among the ranks and she was glad to be working with the boys.

Stuart Hardwicke took over the meeting and walked everyone through the fourteen-day schedule which included a Saturday start with six days on, one day off, six on again, one more off, and then two more days shooting to complete the picture. It wasn't the first time Sheila had worked this low-budget schedule designed around picking up equipment on Friday and returning everything on the Monday two weeks later. She knew the drill. Since the camera, grip, and vehicle rental facilities are closed over the weekends this schedule maximized the two-week rate. She was all too familiar. Top dog gigs start on Mondays. Bottom feeders begin shooting on Saturdays.

Then Stuart began the tedious journey through every page of the script, detailing concerns for each scene, asking the room if there were any questions. The ninety-six-page script took just under two hours. Sheila was incredibly bored and couldn't wait to get out of there. She needed to prep the camera package and she didn't need to be here. This was an incredible waste of time.

Stuart spoke about their accommodations, the historic Gold Strike Lodge. During the winter months, the hotel housed skiers and snowboarders, and he explained, "As luck would have it, there is a hot tub and a mini indoor pool. Bring swimsuits if you got 'em."

The hotel would be closed to guests not working on the film so the production office would be located in the lobby. Housekeeping staff would service rooms only twice a week. A credit card was required at check-in for incidentals. He also informed everyone that, unfortunately, there was no cell phone reception up the hill at the movie ranch location, so they should plan accordingly.

There was a collective moan.

Tami's stylist Diane raised her hand with a question.

"Yes," Stuart said.

"How are we going to check our messages without reception?" she asked.

"You're going to have to wait until the end of the day when you're back down at the hotel," he said, then to everyone Stuart suggested, "which means you'll want to put your phones in airplane mode so the battery doesn't run down searching for a connection all day. A reminder will be in the call sheet."

"You're kidding," Diane replied, clearly not happy.

"I wish I was, but it is what it is," said Stuart.

Diane sat down shaking her head in disgust. Many in the room shifted in their chairs at the thought of not being connected throughout the day.

Finally, Stuart wrapped up the meeting on a stern, downer note reminding all that it was fire season and that smoking anywhere but the designated areas would not be tolerated and would be grounds for immediate dismissal, no exceptions. "This," he added, "is especially important in the Western town since so much of the wood is aged and dry."

Sheila was glad she gave up smoking years ago and didn't have to worry about it.

Lastly, Stuart urged everyone to carpool to the location and detailed maps were provided in their packets. With that, the meeting came to an end.

Thank God.

Sheila made plans to ride up with Giovanni tomorrow afternoon. She gathered her things and was heading off to the camera rental house to prepare the package when Eddie found her. "I'm glad you're on board," he said. She suspected what he really meant was *Maybe we can sleep together again.*

"I thought Chris Sanderson was directing," was all she could think to say.

Sheila could see that she'd struck a nerve. "Nah ... Sanderson's a hack," Eddie said with bravado just before he was interrupted by Stuart.

On the way out, she passed Tami's vanity team, arguing with the young receptionist about validating their parking.

"You've got to be kidding!" Diane said, aghast.

Good luck with that, Sheila thought. *Welcome to the world of bottom feeders.*

CHAPTER ELEVEN

Eddie was given a sealed manila envelope addressed to Susan Pike Casting. "Since you're going over there, give this to Susan, will you?" Sam asked him. "You'll save me the expense of sending a messenger. Make sure Susan gets it."

"Sure thing," Eddie agreed.

"Call me after the session," Sam said. "Fill me in on who your top choices are."

"Sounds good."

"And here," Sam gave Eddie a window envelope with a check inside. "Even though we don't have a signed deal yet, here's a little walking-around money, in good faith, in case you need it."

"Thanks, Sam. Appreciate it." Eddie knew it would take at least a week before his lawyer would get around to looking at his contract, and by then they'd be halfway through principal photography. Eddie was definitely a back-burner client when it came to his lawyer, with little priority because the fees he'd earned were so low. He figured Sam knew that too.

"Don't forget to give Susan that package."

In the elevator Eddie examined the check. It was made out to him for four thousand dollars.

Nice.

Stuck in traffic, curiosity got the best of him. Eddie was certain he could pry open the envelope without anyone knowing, so he did. There were two stacks of hundred-dollar bills bound by bank-issued paper bands—$5,000 each. There was also a note written on a yellow Post-it, "Sue, dear, sorry for the delay," with Sam's familiar chicken-scratch signature. Eddie put it back and resealed the envelope. He had never seen so much cash before. No wonder Sam didn't send a messenger.

Sam had mentioned he was not borrowing from the bank on this movie and that it was funded by investors from back East. This much cash—could these people, whoever they are, be laundering money? Why hadn't Sam given him cash as a start-up fee, as his walking-around money? Cash would have been very cool, and maybe even nontaxable. Eddie figured Sam probably needed a paper trail of his payment as proof to the Directors Guild.

That must be it.

Eddie had heard stories from other directors of movies financed with cash, some of them shot overseas; no 1099 tax forms and no reason to claim the income. Or maybe Susan Pike insisted on cash. It seemed weird.

Susan Pike Casting was in a three-story office building on Magnolia Boulevard in Burbank. The directory in the lobby showed an assortment of small-business tenants: insurance agents, tax accountants, and a few production and music companies. He took the stairs to the top floor. A handful of actors were seated in the reception area studying their lines.

Susan's roly-poly receptionist greeted him and escorted Eddie to the main room. There were balance rails on the walls, and Eddie could see the space doubled as a dance studio. A video camera was set on a flimsy tripod. On the portable table, there were stacks of eight-by-ten headshots and paperwork. Susan Pike, a frizzy-haired, raspy-voiced woman in her fifties, greeted him. He caught the scent of her musky perfume.

"Ed, so wonderful to see you again," she said.

"Susan. How's it going?" he said and they hugged. Eddie handed her the package. "Sam asked me to give you this."

"Oh?" she said, and opened the envelope. He could see her eyes light up when she noted the contents. "I'll be right back," she said, "and then we'll get started. Can I get you anything? Coffee? Water? Diet Coke?"

"No, thank you."

Susan was off and he took a seat on a foldable chair. On the last movie, working with Susan as the casting director, Eddie got the feeling Sam and Susan had known each other for many years, even that they might have slept together. That brought his mind to Sheila. He was glad to see she was in the camera department. That night they'd spent together was really great—the last time he'd been with a woman. *Has it been that long?* They went out to dinner a couple times after but she always found a reason to cut the night short and never came back to his place or invited him to hers. He'd made overtures to plenty of women since, waitresses, even girls he'd met at the track. He'd even taken a few out but nothing sparked with any of them. He could never close the deal.

He'd found himself watching Sheila while she worked, impressed by the way she went about her camera duties, methodical and committed. He picked up on a sense of adventure and fearlessness. She was tomboyish, sure, but at the same time had a laid-back and relaxed femininity. She seemed confident and sure of herself, didn't suffer fools, which he liked. She was from North Carolina, so it made sense—a Southern girl. She could have been the grown-up version of that girl from *To Kill a Mockingbird*. Scout, wasn't that her name? From all the books he was forced to read in school, that was Eddie's favorite.

He and Sheila joked around a lot on that shoot and he'd felt a real connection. Eddie imagined they'd make a great couple. This would be a partner who understood how crazy it is to work in the film and TV industry, a big plus. He knew she was working toward being a cinematographer, so maybe they could work together. But Eddie was so busy directing that movie he'd had little time to get to know her.

Then, at the wrap party downtown in a cool art deco event space that had been one of the locations on that film, both Sheila and Giovanni showed up overdressed for the party but fit right into the space. He wore a vintage tux. She was in heels and a black cocktail dress, had put up her hair, and looked great. Eddie was floored. All the while on set she'd worn jeans and flannel shirts, work clothes which disguised the incredible body she had. Who would have known?

He sensed Sheila felt uncomfortable wearing that revealing dress, not really her style, and Eddie figured that could have been the reason she drank so much. He sensed she and Giovanni weren't dating, but asked her just in case. She admitted Giovanni was gay which didn't come as a surprise, so Eddie devoted the evening to seducing her.

Then back in his apartment, as they stood beside his bed, the moment he couldn't get out of his mind was looking in Sheila's eyes and placing his hands around her slender waist. He remembered feeling the warmth of her hips through the silk fabric. Then to zip down the back of that dress … it made his heart skip just to think about it.

After that night, they went out a few times to sushi restaurants and screenings but she came off cold. He tried to advance the ball but she wouldn't reciprocate. Then she suddenly broke it off. He was heartbroken. He kept trying to reach out but she wouldn't return any of his text messages. Had she blocked him on her phone? *What did I do wrong?*

With Sheila on this film, and away on location, he hoped for an encore performance.

Susan returned and they dove into the tedious casting process—put on the face, meet and greet. He realized, no matter what, his decisions could easily be vetoed by Sam. He'd supply two or three choices for each role and Sam would review the video clips for final say of who to hire. Long ago Eddie realized that television is primarily a producer's medium, not the director's. Sam's name would be on both the opening credits, as executive producer, and then a single card at the very end of the movie would read, "Sam Carver Entertainment."

Eddie knew the game. He was hired to say "Action ... Cut" and take the blame.

* * *

The next morning, after Eddie had washed the Subaru and filled it with gas, he stopped at BevMo to stock up. It was Eddie's tradition while shooting on location to bring a couple of bottles of high-end single-malt scotch to share with the cast and crew. This was the kind of thing legendary director John Huston would do, drink with Bogart or Edward G. Robinson, old-school, holding court and telling stories at the end of the long production day. He also bought some decent beer and tequila plus Margarita mix because he remembered that was what Sheila liked. He went for a half-dozen vodka minis—Ketel One this time, not his regular Popov, since he was flush. The minis were small enough to fit in his pocket to augment either an overpriced drink at the bar or for a clandestine late-in-the-day nip when *the urge* called.

Earlier that morning Sam had emailed him with his choices, having viewed the audition clips overnight. There were only a few actors Eddie would have chosen otherwise, but it all looked good and he'd make it work since there was no time to debate. Susan would make the offers—SAG low-budget minimum plus ten percent for the agent, no doubt.

The drive was peaceful, a calm before the storm. He was

well aware the next two weeks would be a whirlwind of activity, but this was what he lived for. Deep down he knew most show business people, including himself, had a crazy streak in them. It's like they all carried an inkling of a tragic flaw—the flame of a burning dream that couldn't be extinguished. *Why am I drawn to this?* he sometimes wondered.

One night this subject came up while drinking with a veteran director he respected, an old guy who'd navigated countless episodes of seventies and eighties TV crime drama (including *The Rockford Files*, Eddie's all-time favorite). They were bellied up to the bar at Santa Monica's famed Chez Jay, drinking Manhattans after attending the annual American Film Market across the street at the Loews Hotel. "It's like this, kid," the seasoned director had explained to Eddie, "have you ever heard of the Flying Wallendas, the high-wire act?"

"Vaguely," Eddie replied.

"They were fearless, the best ever, and worked without a net. The whole family would stack up in a pyramid and walk the tightrope together. Unbelievable shit, never a net below them, and always a huge draw. Then there was a tragic fall and a bunch of them died. Had they had a net ... but no, that wasn't their style. So in the hospital a bunch of newspaper reporters get to the surviving patriarch laying in traction or something. They ask the poor bastard, 'Mister Wallenda, tell us, you've lost everything ... do you plan to give up the act?' So the guy thinks about it for a moment, and then says, 'Life is the wire, all else is waiting.'"

Eddie so loved that story. It rang so true. Now the waiting part was over. For the next couple of months, until he handed over his director's cut, he would be on the wire and "living the dream" once again. Then sixty days or so later, the *waiting* would begin all over again. Hopefully this film would be a stepping-stone to the next project and open new horizons. That was how it was supposed to work.

Cruising up the mountain road, Eddie first saw the crudely

painted sign that said JERKY 500 FEET before he spotted the white
grip truck pulled over on the shoulder. There was a pickup truck
with a camper shell, its tailgate down, and Giovanni, Sheila, and the
grip-and-gaffer team of Paul and John standing beside an old man
dressed in overalls.

Bingo. Eddie saw this as a perfect opportunity to talk to Sheila.

He parked alongside Giovanni's Land Rover and got out. The
old man's ferocious pit bull, bound by a long leash tied to a tree,
barked at Eddie. The old man hushed his animal with, "Quiet,
Rosie! No barking!"

"What's going on?" Eddie said as he approached, looking
to Sheila for a signal, any kind of warmth or little smile. He got
nothing.

"Checking out the roadside jerky," John said, chewing on a
sample. "It's good, try some."

"Organic beef, buffalo, and turkey," the crusty vendor said.

Eddie sampled a piece. It *was* good. Not too chewy and a little
spicy.

"Got salmon and herring, too. All 100 percent natural with
no MSG, preservatives, or additives. I make it all myself. Name's
Chuck," he said offering his hand.

Eddie greeted the old guy with a shake. He could feel callouses on
the man's meaty palm. "I'm Eddie. Nice to meet you," he returned.
He could see Chuck had plenty of character with a sun-weathered
face and deep-blue eyes framed by muttonchop sideburns.

"Anyone ever call you Fast Eddie?" asked Chuck. "Like the pool
player in that movie?"

"You mean Paul Newman, *The Color of Money*?" Eddie asked.

"No. *The Hustler*, with Jackie Gleason."

"Oh, Eddie's fast all right," Sheila said with a wry smile, "real
fast, but more like Ed Wood or Roger Corman."

Paul and John burst out laughing.

"Who?" Chuck asked.

"They're just razzing me," Eddie said, smiling at Sheila. *Good one.*

"Y'all really making a movie?" asked Chuck.

"Up at the Crescent Movie Ranch," said Paul.

"I read the Louis L'Amour Western paperbacks. Robert J. Randisi too. Those ones are good. And Michael Zimmer, him too. Got a few in my truck."

Eddie said, "That's great. If you're interested in being an extra, we could probably work you in."

"An extra? What's that?"

"You'd be in the background, as one of the townsfolk, or something along those lines," Eddie explained.

"No starring role?" Chuck teased.

"Unfortunately, no. We've already cast those parts."

"What's so *extra* about it?" asked Chuck.

"That's what background artists are called," Eddie explained. "Don't know why, but they are. If you're interested, give us your number and we'll let you know what day we could use you. No promises, but you might get a few bucks for the effort, or at the very least a hot lunch."

"Should I bring my Winchester?" he asked, nodding to his truck. "Got me a trusty lever-action thirty-thirty like my namesake, Chuck Conners."

"Who?"

"You know, *The Rifleman.*"

"Please, no firearms," Eddie said. "There are no guns in our movie. It's about miners and we're making a family film."

"Okay then." Chuck seemed disappointed.

"How can we reach you?"

"Here," Chuck said, handing him the grease-stained paper insert from inside one of the jerky packages. "Phone number is on there. And the address for the website my grandkids made for me, too." Rosie started barking again, distracting Chuck, who excused himself to calm the agitated dog.

"What do you think?" Eddie asked Giovanni.

"He's got a very interesting face, no? Maybe we feature him in the foreground, doing some business with horse tack or something, then we track off to reveal the scene. Huh?"

"Sounds good."

Chuck returned after giving his dog some of the jerky to quiet her. Paul and John bought a handful of packs each then everyone climbed back into their vehicles.

Other than Sheila's snide comment about Ed Wood, affectionately known as the world's worst director of all time and a transvestite, and prolific B-movie king Roger Corman, Eddie picked up no other signals from her, no additional glances, nothing. And her comment about being fast, could that have been a reference to sex?

He remembered their night together and the feel of the inside of her soft thighs. *Had I come too fast? Probably.* Eddie couldn't help it. She was too sexy. *Damn.*

On the drive up the hill, Eddie strategized on how he could best reengage Sheila and make her realize they'd make an awesome couple. She'd surely be the cure to his loneliness and depression. He'd walk the line and wouldn't drink so much. She'd curb his tendency toward self-destruction. He'd take care of her and have something to live for. *What had I done wrong?* he pondered again. *What can I do now to make things right?*

* * *

The Gold Strike Lodge was a rustic hotel with a log-cabin facade. Eddie parked around back. He could see the place had touristy charm with its vintage black iron mining implements tacked up on the wood siding. It reminded him of Knott's Berry Farm before they brought in all the roller coasters and thrill rides.

Once Eddie entered the hotel, he came across Tami's vanity team—Connie, Bonnie, and Diane—standing beside their bags with a look of terror in their eyes, as if they had just seen a ghost.

"What's the matter?" he asked.

"We can't stay here," Diane snapped. "Tami can't stay here!"

"What's the problem?" he asked her just as he caught sight of Stuart Hardwicke pacing near the stone fireplace while speaking on his cell phone, apparently dealing with this crisis.

"These poor animals," Diane said. "It's disgusting."

Eddie considered the dozens of taxidermy displays throughout the lobby, birds and furry critters on the walls, a few of them perched on pedestals. There was even a grizzly bear up on its hind legs behind the counter.

Diane seethed, "Don't you people realize Tami is the founding member of Animal Stance?"

"I, uh ..." Eddie stammered.

"We can't let her see this!" Connie exclaimed before the three women grabbed their designer luggage and charged out.

From across the lobby, Stuart offered Eddie a shrug. Who knew?

CHAPTER
TWELVE

Tom drove to location, fighting a cold.

He was scheduled to start work tomorrow, the first day of principal photography, but today he was technically on the clock, a travel day, and getting paid to simply drive up to the mountains, check into the hotel, and report to wardrobe for a final fitting. He loaded himself up with Alka-Seltzer Plus before he made the two-and-a-half-hour journey.

Tom's agent had emailed him the actors' production schedule known within the industry as the "day out of days." He was disappointed to see he was in and out in seven days which, as he knew from years in the business, meant he'd be paid for one full workweek plus a single day. If the production schedule had permitted just one extra day, even a travel day, SAG guidelines mandated Tom should be paid for the entire second week. That would boil down to another fifteen hundred dollars or so, at least. He so hoped this film would run over schedule. *We'll see.*

Working the system came with experience.

Tom had banked considerable overtime on previous jobs by

keeping a watchful eye on the clock. He'd even purposely slowed down at the end of the day, blowing a take now and again, or tying up the director with cerebral discussions about his character motivations in order to milk lucrative overtime. Of course, he was careful to make the delays feel random, never appearing to be *his* fault as to blemish his professional reputation.

On one independent film, knowing the fifteen-plus hour day was well into costly overtime, referred to in the industry as *Golden Time*, Tom threw the inept, frazzled wardrobe department under the bus by purposely dressing in the wrong clothes. Then, on set, he came off as the hero when he pretended to discover the mistake. The wardrobe change followed by makeup touch-ups bought him another hour on the clock. Because they were so into overtime by that point it all boiled down to two hundred bucks more.

Tom planned on bleeding this production too.

He pulled up to the Gold Strike Lodge and made a point to jot down his mileage, another way to pad the bill. He checked himself in the mirror to make sure his thinning hair was just right. The mirror did not lie; Tom was balding. He wondered if hair plugs might help him get more roles. He examined his teeth for peppers and such since he had eaten a panini sandwich on the way up, then he grabbed his bags.

Passing a large horse trailer, he could smell manure. A horse's eye stared at him though a vent. It was creepy and gave him a chill.

Then *the wave* came.

He'd felt it before, always at times before something horrible happened, before earthquakes, car accidents, even before deaths of friends and family. It was a strange and awkward feeling, a premonition. His butt puckered and his tongue felt bloated. His fingers tingled and he felt nauseous. He dropped his bags and steadied himself on the fender of a pickup, considered driving back to Los Angeles. *That wouldn't be good. I would disappoint Tami. I didn't have to audition.*

He stood beside the horse trailer for a moment until the feeling passed. Maybe the queasiness was brought on by that cold medicine. Or maybe it was something in that spicy sandwich, soured chipotle mayonnaise or something. To make matters even worse, he saw what looked like an aquarium in the cab of the pickup with snakes coiled inside atop seat-cover upholstery resembling an Indian blanket.

"Can I help you?" a man said, coming around the back of the trailer. He wore dirty jeans and cowboy boots. Tom figured he was probably the owner of the pickup truck he was leaning on.

"No, I'm good," Tom said. "Just checking out the ponies."

"Don't put your fingers in there. Patches can be ornery. Might mistake it for a carrot and take a bite."

"Wouldn't think of it."

"Jimmy, lead wrangler," the man said and offered his hand.

Tom returned the greeting. "Tom Birch, I'm one of the actors."

"Glad to meet ya," Jimmy said. "You gonna ride a horse in this movie?"

"I don't think so ... maybe."

"What character do you play?"

"Bartholomew."

Jimmy scrunched his sunburned face as he tried to remember. "I don't recall a ..."

"The proprietor of the general store. I think I ride a carriage," Tom said.

Jimmy snapped his finger, pointed to Tom and said, "That's right, you're the dandy."

"Dandy?" Tom questioned.

"The dude."

A scrawny guy wearing ragged jeans emerged from the hotel and Jimmy said to him, "Lucky, help me with the tack." Turning back to Tom, Jimmy said, "Excuse me, partner, nice meeting you," and he went about their business.

The dandy?

Tom grabbed his bags and continued into the hotel. The lobby was a buzz of activity. Assorted crewmembers were in meetings, equipment cases were clustered in one corner, and techs were setting up a copy machine in the other. There was nobody to greet him, so he moved to registration.

Upon check-in he asked the teenage girl behind the counter, young enough to make him wonder why she wasn't in school, "Which room is Tami in?"

She informed him that Tami was not staying at the hotel.

"Oh? Where then?"

"In a cabin up the road from here."

Tom was disappointed. He wondered who else got special treatment.

"Why aren't you in school?" he asked the young girl.

"I'm homeschooled," she said.

"That any good?" asked Tom.

"You got a problem with that?" she said, as if accused.

"No. I'm just asking because I'm a teacher," he said.

"My aunt Lilly is my teacher."

"That's nice," Tom said. The encounter made him think about the script and the scene that featured Tami's character orating to the townspeople. Her monologue was about the mining company exploiting their children with low wages and keeping them out of school. Although he had no lines, Tom was in that scene, reacting to her speech. He hadn't decided yet how he'd play it—how he'd react to Tami's passionate plea.

His room was acceptable, nothing special, with a view of the mountains, so there was no need to call his agent and complain. He unpacked his things and replaced the always-questionable hotel bedspread with one he'd brought from home. This was a practice he'd fallen into years ago. After his socks were tucked neatly in the drawer and his pants and shirts hung, Tom went back downstairs and reported to the wardrobe department.

Wardrobe was crammed into a cluttered conference room in

the basement of the hotel. Linda, the costume designer he'd met in LA when he went in for measurements, greeted him and gave him a plain, dark wool suit with a string bow tie. Putting it on, Tom began to imagine the character traits he might experiment with while playing the role, maybe a slight swagger in his gait. The wool made him itch. An assortment of cowboy hats on the racks caught his attention.

"Do I get to wear a hat?" he asked Linda, on her knees and hemming his pants at the cuffs.

"No. Eddie thinks your character wouldn't wear a hat."

"Oh yeah?"

"Bartholomew is more of a townie rather than a ranch hand," she said.

"I want a hat," he said, thinking it would be a good way to cover his battle with male pattern baldness.

"Hmm … how about this," she said, stood and produced a rounded bowler.

He tried it on. "Doesn't fit," he said, even though it did.

"I'll talk to Eddie," she said.

"Where is Ed?"

"Probably up on set," she said. "Now let's pick some boots."

Linda ducked behind the racks of clothing as Tom checked himself out in the mirror. He hadn't met the director, but he really wanted a cowboy hat.

CHAPTER **THIRTEEN**

Sheila dropped her bags off in her room before boarding the production shuttle idling outside the Gold Strike. She checked her phone to make sure she didn't have to return any emails or texts since she remembered there'd be no connection up the hill. Roland hadn't called or texted again, not since last night, and there were no new voice mails. She hadn't heard from her roommate Lisa at all, and that really hurt. They'd been close friends, or so Sheila thought. She'd trusted Lisa completely, like the sister Sheila never had. Where's Lisa's apology? Where's her explanation of what happened? In a way it hurt even more than Roland's betrayal. Everyone knows men are pigs, but Lisa? Unbelievable. The anger burned. Sheila hadn't replied to him, and didn't plan to, but was curious how long he would persist.

A handful of other crewmembers filled out the vehicle, most of whom she recognized from yesterday's production meeting. Stressed-out Assistant Director Stuart Hardwicke boarded, manila envelope in hand, and said, "Don, swing by the Tami compound on the way up and drop this off for me, will ya?"

"Shouldn't be a problem," driver Don said and the van set out.

Don was a potbellied, middle-aged ruffian wearing a sweat-stained Kenworth cap. *Typical Teamster.* Even though this movie was nonunion, and not employing actual Teamster drivers, Sheila knew many of these guys carried union cards in their overstuffed wallets but took nonunion work when they could get it, just as she had. And because drivers on film and TV tend to sit around drinking coffee, reading the newspaper, and playing cards while everyone else was working, Teamsters had become the brunt of many inside jokes.

Her favorite joke came one night working late on a legit TV pilot on the Fox lot. At the end of the day, a veteran soundman posed a question while she was filling out her time card on the camera truck. He held up one of the driver employment forms with its iconic Teamster logo on it, an illustrated circular badge crowned by two horse heads, and asked, "Do you know why the logo for the International Brotherhood of Teamsters has horses on it?" Sheila had remembered seeing this logo tattooed on a Teamster's arm when she first came to Hollywood and guessed, "Something to do with hitching up a team of horses?"

"Wrong," the no-nonsense soundman informed, "It's because no other mammal on earth sleeps standing up."

Too funny. Every time she'd seen the Hollywood Teamster's union logo after that day she'd always thought of that joke. Driver Don was no exception, another bottom feeder working for Carver Entertainment's meager, nonunion day rate. *Welcome to the club.*

It was a curvy drive up the hill with an uneven road and sharp turns. Sitting in the back seat, Sheila felt a hint of car sickness. After ten minutes or so, Don turned off the main road and up the driveway of an impressive mountain chalet. The French Country–styled home had an impressive porch and hot tub off its redwood deck. It was the kind of place she'd fantasized about; a cozy mountain hideaway, the perfect place to spend a magical Christmas with loved ones, like something out of a romance novel. She imagined what the cabin might look like covered by a light dusting of snow.

Don jumped out and knocked on the door. Sheila saw it open a crack and he passed the envelope inside. Then he returned to the passenger van and they continued up the hill.

The pavement transitioned to a rutted dirt road. The bumpy washboard rattled the vehicle so much that the plastic interior of the coach squeaked with annoyance. This only added to Sheila's feeling of queasiness. She tried her best to suppress it, wondering why she felt so nauseous.

Could I be pregnant? Impossible. Or is it?

She tried to calculate the last time she and Roland made love, but then remembered that she'd had her period when she was back home dealing with her mom. *Thank God.*

Finally, they arrived at the movie ranch, a rickety collection of Western facades spread out among an uneven dirt road. It was less impressive than she'd imagined. Everyone got out of the shuttle and went about their business. Sheila remembered to put her phone on airplane mode to save battery life as she strolled to base camp. Stuart had suggested that. She opened the camera truck and got right to work, organizing the shelves and preparing the equipment for the next day.

Luther, the stoner kid Giovanni hired as their second assistant cameraman, arrived from LA in a literal cloud of dust, his Mini Cooper sliding sideways and kicking up dirt as it came to a stop.

Shit! She closed the camera cases as the plume of dirt wafted into the truck. Since dust poses a major problem for the camera department, Sheila was pissed. Her battle against the fine particles that cling to lenses and jam equipment had already begun, thanks to stupid Luther. She knew there would be a lot of dust on this show but didn't expect so much of it so soon.

"Dumb shit!"

"What?" he said getting out of the car.

"Kick up more dust next time, why don't ya?" she snapped at him.

"Sorry," Luther said, eyes downcast, a loping hangdog. Sheila sensed he wasn't the sharpest crayon in the box. She suspected

Giovanni had hired Luther because he had *the look*. Giovanni either had a crush on him or they were in a relationship, she didn't know. She'd only worked with him once before and hadn't picked up any nonverbal cues that they were romantically involved, so the verdict was still out. All she knew was that Giovanni liked having one or two really good-looking guys around. Luther would be the eye candy on this job. Dumb maybe, but she couldn't deny he was easy to look at.

He opened the back seat of his car and carried two lens cases to the truck. With a grunt he hoisted the cases onto the liftgate. "I've been calling," he said, "your phone off?"

"There's no reception up here on set," she said.

"You're kidding?" he said with concern and pulled his iPhone from his pocket to confirm.

"Wish I was kidding. It's ridiculous."

"They nixed the prime lenses," Luther said, brushing the blond bangs out of his eyes.

"What?"

"Apparently once they saw the bid from the camera house some genius in the production office decided to drop the box of primes to save money. All we've got are these two zooms," he said, pushing the cases further onto the liftgate.

"Giovanni agreed to that?" she asked.

"Don't know. Where is he?"

She needed to talk to Giovanni about this immediately. Sheila grabbed the broom and tossed it to Luther. Not quick enough to catch it, the wooden handle smacked him in the forehead.

"Sweep out the truck," she said, jumping off the tailgate.

Searching for Giovanni, she first walked through base camp where the trucks and trailers were staged. Sheila was taken aback by the size of the vanity department for such a low-budget movie, with their seemingly brand-new wardrobe and makeup trailer. Meanwhile, the camera department, she lamented, was crammed into a rinky-dink old and clunky cube truck she'd have to share with the jokers from the sound department. And now no prime lenses?

Where are the priorities?

Sheila walked past Tami's vanity team, all wearing yoga pants. They had retro disco music playing and were casually loading supplies into their shiny new trailer. Makeup kits, folded towels, assorted cases, and wardrobe steamers—*no expense spared there.* Sheila was surprised to see the younger Diane do the heavy lifting by hoisting what appeared to be a barber chair into the trailer while Connie and Bonnie stood by and supervised, sipping bottled Evian water. *Why don't they help?* Sheila wondered. *What's with these women?*

She could see Giovanni was not at base camp, so she headed up to the Western town. On the way up the hill, beyond the horizon, she could see the smoke from a distant forest fire. Having lived in Southern California over the years, this wasn't an uncommon sight. She figured the dry Santa Ana winds were probably fanning the flames, making it worse, and she hoped smoke in the upper atmosphere wouldn't make the natural daylight hard to match from shot to shot.

She headed toward the bustle of activity surrounding the general store set. Art department guys were unloading barrels, furniture, and horse troughs from the prop truck. She saw Giovanni inside the store with director Eddie. It appeared as though they were planning the next day's coverage. When Giovanni caught sight of her, she motioned him to come out. He gave her a signal to hold on, and after a few minutes he finished his discussion and met her on the splintered wooden sidewalk.

"Got a second?" she asked.

"Sure," Giovanni said. Sheila led him out of earshot from the others and waited on the piercing sound of a circular saw before she informed him, "Production nixed the prime lenses. All we have are two zooms."

"Yes, I know. I agreed to that."

"Why?"

"Sam is cutting every corner. It was either we do that or we go only with a doorway dolly. I let Eddie decide."

"Okay then," she said, "so that's how it's going to be." It was *so* wrong. She wanted to ask him if he had seen the size of the vanity department trailers but refrained, not wanting to sound negative.

At that moment Eddie stepped up and acknowledged her. "Hey, Sheila," he said brightly.

"Eddie," she responded as neutral as she could, an attempt to give him the signal she was not interested. Then, turning to Giovanni, she said, "I just had to make you aware."

"Aware of what?" Eddie asked.

"No prime lenses, only zooms. What we talked about," Giovanni said to Eddie.

"Oh …"

"Thanks, Sheila. We'll make do," Giovanni said.

She nodded and turned to go, sensing Eddie's eyes on her.

Walking back down the hill, she came upon the camera truck and could see Luther lying flat, sprawled facedown on the floor of the truck.

He motioned her to get down.

Sheila was confused.

He waved his arms again and said, "Get down! Get down!"

At first she thought it was a joke, but from the expression on his face she could see he was serious. She hunched low and approached.

"Someone shot at me!"

"What?"

"They shot the truck," Luther said, clearly shaken.

Sheila squatted and scanned the dry meadow but saw nothing. "When?"

"Just a minute ago," he said. "I heard a loud pop. All of a sudden sunlight was pouring in through a hole above my head."

She reached for her cell phone to call Giovanni but remembered it didn't work. She scanned the surroundings again.

"I'm making a break for it," he said.

"Wait. Give me a second." Sheila jumped up on the tailgate and examined the inside of the truck. There was indeed a hole, about the size of a quarter, sunlight streaming through. She ran her finger along the jagged edge. Fragments of fiberglass and particleboard came off, floating in the beam illuminated as a single shard of sunlight.

Following the trajectory, there was no hole on the other side of the truck but rather a black shaft imbedded into the metallic strut side panel. She gave it a yank and it came loose. The arrowhead, four-pointed and razor-sharp, gave her pause. And there were two pop-out blades behind the pointy nose blade. It appeared the rear blades were designed to spring out upon impact. "Who'd you piss off?" she asked.

"That an arrow?"

"Looks like."

Sheila examined it closer. There appeared to be Vaseline on the razor-tip. *What the hell?*

"Indians?" Luther wondered aloud, hunched, scanning the meadow.

CHAPTER FOURTEEN

Eddie turned his palms up and said, "Really? Ten extras? You've got to be kidding."

"Yes, Eddie, ten," Stuart replied, double-checking the notes in his thick binder. "That's what's we've scheduled for tomorrow."

"That's crazy. I need twenty, at least."

"You can't have twenty."

"Why not?"

"Not in the budget, my friend. You've got to make do."

"But we've got all the town exteriors tomorrow."

"I realize that."

"Then you're going to have to dress the production assistants in wardrobe and work them in."

"We can't do that."

"Then get me more extras."

"Realize there are other big days. Whatever I book tomorrow will take away from—"

Eddie could hear the radio squawk, audible through the production headset Stuart was wearing. Stuart held up his hand

and turned away, breaking conversation midsentence, caught up in a communication Eddie couldn't hear.

"Go for Stuart," he said into the speaker, and then after a few seconds, "Roger that, Sam. He's standing right next to me." Stuart mouthed "Sam," unplugged the headset, and wrestled the black radio off his belt. He held out the walkie-talkie.

Eddie took the radio and pushed the talk button, "What's up Sam?"

"Tami asked to have dinner with you tonight," Sam sounded.

Eddie cringed. There was so much to do; finalize wardrobe, revise his shot list, go over the video for the children roles, and now fight for more extras. But he also realized if he refused the invitation it might alienate the star of his film.

"Eddie, you there?" Sam asked.

"I'm always available for Tami," Eddie forced himself to say.

"Fantastic. I'll have a driver pick you up from base camp. Say in about thirty minutes?"

"Sounds good, Sam," Eddie said, already regretting the decision. He handed the radio back to Stuart.

"What's Tami like?" Stuart asked. "Think she's going to be cool?"

"She's okay, I guess," he said, hoping she wouldn't be too needy. He didn't have time for any of that.

"I know we had our differences on the last film," Stuart said. "But I consider that water under the bridge. We're in the same boat here, you and I, and we both know this one's going to be a challenge. Sam has made it clear my job is to guarantee we stay on schedule."

"I'm totally with ya, Stu, and Sam and I are in agreement too, and we *will not* go over budget. But realize we're making a movie here, not a schedule."

"Ooh, that hurt," Stuart said with a hand to his heart, as if pained by the assault on his artistic integrity.

"All I'm saying is allow yourself to be flexible," Eddie continued. "Just because something's in your paperwork doesn't mean—"

Eddie heard communication on the radio again and Stuart held his palm out, essentially giving Eddie "the hand" to halt him from completing his point. After a few seconds, Stuart said, "I'm on my way." He turned to Eddie. "Can we walk and talk?"

Eddie sensed the urgency and asked, "What's up?"

"Someone shot an arrow at the camera truck. The sheriff's here."

* * *

Descending the hill alongside Stuart, Eddie could see the San Bernardino County Deputy Sheriff cruiser and a Fish & Game SUV by the camera truck. A cluster of crewmembers including Sheila, Giovanni, and Don were huddled near the liftgate. As Eddie and Stuart arrived, Luther was in the midst of explaining what happened to a small-framed female officer complete with wide-brimmed hat, aviator sunglasses, and tooled, black leather gun belt perched high.

The Fish & Game officer, a potbellied and bearded guy wearing considerably fewer accessories, held an arrow in his latex-gloved hand.

"I didn't see anybody," Luther explained. "I thought it was a gunshot at first so I got down real low."

"How about you?" Deputy Martinez asked Sheila.

"I wasn't here when it happened, and I didn't see anyone either," she said. "After I found the arrow I pulled it out and noticed there was some sort of weird grease on the tip."

The deputy glanced at the arrow in the game warden's hand. He sniffed the tip and confirmed it. "Petroleum jelly. Bowhunters are known to lubricate arrowheads to make them more deadly, for deeper penetration."

"How deadly are they?" Stuart asked.

"These modern compound bows," the warden said, "can fire an arrow up to four hundred feet per second."

"Which means?"

"One arrow can take down a moose."

"Seriously? A moose?" Stuart questioned.

"The technology behind these new graphite bows, with their pulleys and cams …" he said to everyone, "they're incredibly powerful weapons, quite deadly. And combined with the design of these newfangled broadheads …" he said, pointing the stainless steel tip. "Considerable killing power, I'm afraid."

The deputy pulled up her belt and asked Stuart, "And you are?"

"Stuart Hardwicke, unit management, first assistant director."

Eddie thought *unit management* was an odd choice of words. As always, Stuart felt the need to endorse his own authority.

"Assistant director … is that like an assistant manager?" the deputy asked.

Eddie stifled a laugh. *Exactly.*

"I'm in charge of the cast and crew's safety," Stuart said.

"Where were you when this occurred?" she questioned, all business.

"Up on set," Stuart said, thumbing over his shoulder.

"If you're the assistant director, then who's the director?"

"I am, Eddie Lyons," Eddie said and put out his hand.

"Deputy Sondra Martinez," said Sondra with a shake. "Give me a second." She moved around the truck, turned, and scanned the meadow beyond.

Everyone watched in silence.

The game warden asked, "Could someone have been crossed, maybe on the road up here, maybe a person cut off by one of your trucks or something? Or for some reason did somebody get angry at you guys?"

Sheila glanced to Luther who shrugged back, *not me.*

"I'll ask around." Stuart offered.

Deputy Martinez marched out into the dried weeds. With her eyes scanning the earth, Eddie assumed she was looking for footprints.

"Crazy," Eddie said to the others. "Who would shoot an arrow at the camera truck?"

"Any of the equipment damaged?" Giovanni asked.

"I don't think so," Sheila replied.

"Maybe I can patch that hole," Don the driver said, eyeing the punctured fiberglass.

Deputy Martinez returned and asked for a list of everybody in the "production company's employ." Stuart was quick to produce a cast and crew list from his thick binder and handed it to her.

"Everyone should be here, with contact info," Stuart explained. "Do you need to see our permit?"

"Permit?"

"Our film permit."

"This will do for now," Deputy Martinez said. Then, to all, she announced, "If anyone sees anything out of the ordinary, please report it. A stranger hanging around or something a little off … anything. Trust your instincts. Nothing is too small. Is that understood?"

There were nods all around and murmurs of agreement.

"Thank you for your time," she said. "Please be safe."

As the crew dispersed, Deputy Martinez said to the warden, "Bag it. We'll compare this one to the arrows from that roadside kill."

"What roadside kill?" Eddie asked.

"A business traveler encountered arrows while he was changing a flat tire."

"Encountered?"

"Yes. He was shot."

"Near here?" asked Eddie.

"Up around Lake Arrowhead," she said. Turning to Stuart, she handed him her business card. "If anyone reports anything out of the ordinary, or if you have any ideas who may have done this, please don't hesitate to call."

"Will do," Stuart confirmed, stuffing the card in his breast pocket.

She eyed the trees again, "Good luck with your movie. And please, be safe."

Eddie liked her no-nonsense style and watched as she climbed into her squad car and drove off down the hill. The game warden followed.

Eddie stuck around to wait for Don's shuttle to drive him down the hill to Tami's cabin. Lucky approached from behind the truck. "Excuse me, Mr. Lyons," the bony assistant wrangler said, "do you have a minute?"

Lucky's teeth were horribly discolored and Eddie wondered if chewing tobacco was the cause, or possibly extended meth use. He'd seen pictures of addicts on the internet, showing the decaying phases of addiction. "Please, call me 'Eddie,'" he said.

"I was just wondering," Lucky began, "if you'd consider snakes in your movie."

"Snakes?" Eddie questioned, cautious.

"Yes sir. I'm told they're not necessarily in the script—haven't read it yet—but I brought a few along just in case. I mentioned them at the production meeting in LA."

"You brought snakes?"

"Rescue snakes," Lucky said, beaming. He scratched at a scab on his forearm before opening the passenger-side door of his rusty, 1960s-era Ford pickup. A glass aquarium sat in the middle of the truck's bench seat. Empty cigarette packs cluttered the floor. "These babies were abandoned by their previous owner. I rescued them from being destroyed by the government."

"The government?"

"The County. You know … the people at the dog pound. Animal Control. I've got plenty more back home. Lizards too, and piranhas."

Eddie asked, "Why would you bring snakes?"

"To get them in the movie, plus keep an eye on them since they're new," Lucky said, as if it was the most obvious thing in the world. "Reptiles are my hobby and my snakes have been in a bunch of movies and reality TV shows. You can use 'em for free. No charge to the production whatsoever. Just give me credit, that's all I ask. On one movie, I worked with the second unit director and filmed one of my pythons eating a mouse."

Eddie peered into the cab to see the diamond-patterned snakes coiled in a ball within the glass aquarium. One of them moved. "What kind of snakes are these?" he asked.

"Mojave Reds," Lucky said, then lovingly added, "the most lethal rattlesnake in North America."

"You brought rattlesnakes?!"

"They won't bite."

Suddenly Jimmy came up behind them and barked, "Lucky, what the hell are you doing?"

"Showing the director my snakes," he said.

"There's no need for snakes in this movie," Jimmy snapped. "Leave the man alone."

"I was just—"

"I know what you were doing," Jimmy barked. "Why the hell did you bring those fucking things anyway? Nobody wants your snakes. They'll scare the horses."

"I had to."

"That's bullshit. Get them the hell out of here."

"Okay, then, no big deal," Lucky said, relenting.

Eddie could see Lucky was hurt and said, "Thanks, Lucky, but I really don't see a need for snakes in the movie. It's a family film. It's for TV."

"Yes, sir, I understand, but it's also a Western. If you wanted some extra danger somewhere you could always—"

"The man doesn't want your damn snakes!" Jimmy snapped.

Lucky nodded, gently closed the door of the pickup. "Okay, no snakes then."

After the dejected Lucky slinked off, Jimmy confided with Eddie, "Sorry about that. Lucky is crazy about his snakes and reptiles."

"Everyone's got a passion," Eddie said.

"Yeah maybe … but those things give me the creeps. He could have brought harmless garden snakes, but no, instead he carts around rattlesnakes and brags to everyone about how lethal they are."

"How lethal are they?"

"I don't know. He says the baby snakes are the worst."

"How's that?"

"Something about releasing too much venom when they bite, shooting their entire wad. It's especially weird at feeding time."

"What do they eat?"

"Live mice. He brought those too. Look, I'm sorry. I'll make sure he gets those things out of here."

"Don't leave them in the hotel. I won't be able to sleep if I think there are snakes slinking around inside the Gold Strike."

Jimmy laughed. "We'll keep the things locked up in his truck. They can't overheat because they're snakes, right?"

The shuttle van pulled up and Don stuck his head out the window. "You ready, chief?" he asked Eddie.

A welcome distraction, Eddie excused himself.

"I'll take care of it," Jimmy promised before returning to the horses.

Don drove Eddie down the hill and dropped him off outside Tami's cabin. Don said, "Cell phones don't work up here either, so when you want to be picked up, there's a landline in the house. Give the production office a ring and I'll come get ya."

Eddie thanked him and got out. Don lit a cigarette then drove off before Eddie approached the house and knocked on the door.

Tami's stylist Diane answered with, "Hey." She wore tight blue jeans and a beaded Native American–styled top which showed off her toned, muscular arms. He could see she was fit, figured she must work out regularly. Her hair was wet and slicked back, evidence of a recent shower.

"Diane," he said.

She sized him up and said, "Hey."

"Nice digs."

"Yeah," she said nonchalant.

He thought of how freaked out she was back at the Gold Strike with all the taxidermy on the walls. This place felt modern and she appeared at ease.

"Come on in," she said.

He followed her through the foyer, past an antique grandfather clock perched on the landing, and into the kitchen where Tami, Connie, and Bonnie were thumbing through an oversized black-leather artist portfolio. He recognized it from the production meeting back in Los Angeles.

"Eddie, thank you for coming," Tami said, giving him a light hug. "Prestress bonding is always a good idea, don't you agree? I hope you're hungry."

"Thank you for having me." Tami was wearing another one of her casual yet expensive-looking outfits. This one featured hand-stitched floral patterns and reminded him of something the young ingénue would wear in a Bollywood musical. Always in a unique getup; if nothing else, Tami had style.

"We were just going over Diane's book," Tami said. "Come take a look."

Eddie joined them. It was a photo series of models in a country house setting. They posed near a barn, at a pump well, and around an old rusty tractor. The fashion trended toward hippie-chick, but there was disco style in there too. Some of it bordered on semierotic.

Diane explained her inspiration. "I went for seventies glam juxtaposed against the traditional Sadie Hawkins tradition," she said. "Considering the seventies was the peak of the sexual revolution, I worked toward unbridled freedom and combined it with the down-home comfort of a Sadie Hawkins' Day dance, with its acceptable gender swap, the country girl taking charge and asking the boy out on the date for a change."

"Love the boots," Bonnie said.

Eddie felt obliged to compliment and said, "These images are great. I can smell the apple pie cooling in the farmhouse kitchen window."

"Thank you," Diane said stroking her wet hair. "Coming from a big-time director, I'm flattered."

Eddie was about to say he was not a big-time director, not by any stretch, but Tami asked what he'd like to drink. To be polite he said, "Whatever you're having." She chose a Perrier and poured him a glass over ice. He would have much preferred an adult beverage but since nobody else was drinking, Eddie figured, *When in Rome.* The bubbly effervescence tasted bitter and tickled his nose.

As Connie and Bonnie finished preparing the main course, which Eddie learned was eggplant couscous, Diane put her portfolio away and Tami and Eddie had a seat on the couch in the living room. The tasteful interior was Western-themed with Native American art and bronze sculptures of bucking broncos. Tami explained that Connie and Bonnie had been with her on a number of projects. Diane had just joined her team as a consultant to help establish Tami's new "brand."

Eddie recalled Sam complaining about having to employ Tami's expensive entourage. He secretly wished Sam would drop in and add a dash of testosterone to the gathering, hopefully with a bottle of wine.

After what seemed like an eternity, dinner was served. It was clear a lot of time was spent on the presentation of the meal. The main entrée was artistically stacked with a colorful accent sauce and shaved herbs had been sprinkled over the plate. Low fat and healthy no doubt, maybe even vegan and gluten free. Eddie didn't know but could only assume. After sampling it, Eddie wished more effort had gone into the taste of it all. The conversation revolved around Animal Stance, Tami's nonprofit rescue effort, and her promotion of habitat protection and conservation. Eddie was bored.

After dinner, Tami's team cleared the plates and went to work on dessert. This left Tami and Eddie sitting at the table alone. Bonnie changed the dinner music to an opera.

"There's been something I wanted to talk to you about," Tami said. She looked at him with complete seriousness. It was as if she was waiting all this time to drop bad news and had orchestrated the others to give them privacy.

"Yes?" Eddie said and wondered where this was going.

"Before you were involved in this project, when I was working with Chris Sanderson developing the novel into a screenplay, Carver Entertainment agreed to produce, and we were thrilled. But Sam insisted we cut a scene. I agreed at the time but the more I think about it the more I feel that was a grave mistake. I regret that I made that compromise because I feel the scene is so crucial now. The audience really needs to understand why my character is so passionate about her cause."

"Hmm," Eddie responded, encouraging her to continue with, "go on."

"Chris and I planned to speak with Sam about it," Tami said, "and convince him we need to put the scene back in, but then Chris, as you know, had a scheduling conflict and, well ..."

"I see," Eddie said. "What's the scene?"

"It's a flashback, when my character is back in Boston, really a defining moment for her."

A flashback? Boston?

"It's a rainy night," she continued, "and I'm with my mother, in our coach, and we're on the way to the opera, Puccini's *Tosca*," she said.

Mother? There's no mother in the script. A coach? What movie is she talking about?

"We're passing over Boston's cobblestone streets, the scene illuminated by flickering gas lamps, the sound of plodding hooves echoing in the damp streets. We round a corner and come across a building on fire, an old garment factory, a sweatshop. Its workers are pathetically fighting the flames with buckets of water."

Fire and rain? That means hiring special effects technicians. Sweatshop workers? I can barely get ten background extras for tomorrow.

Tami went on with, "My mother barks to our driver to turn the carriage around, but I see a small figure huddled on a stoop. It's a young girl, face blackened with soot." Eddie could see Tami paused in what seemed like a well-timed, calculated play for dramatic effect.

"How young?" Eddie asked, just to say something and fill the gap.

"Seven or eight, a peasant girl, scrawny and malnourished."

You've got to be kidding.

Tami continued. "So I jump out, stomp through the mud, ruining my lace evening gown. I use my shawl to wipe her face. The girl can hardly talk, barely able to breathe. Her lungs have been scorched by the ungodly smoke. I ask her where her parents are. She points to the burning building. I ask what school she goes to, hoping to find someone to help her. She tells me she's never been to school, that she lives and works in the sweatshop. It's all she's ever known. Don't you get it? Much like the children in the mining town, this girl has been exploited, her childhood and life robbed by pure greed."

"I see," he said, trying his best to appear receptive to the idea.

"Then she coughs uncontrollably," Tami said, "she grabs hold of my hand, her eyes flutter, and she ... dies." Tami took another dramatic pause, sat up as if cradling the dead child, and added with emotion in her tone, "I turn to the building, grief stricken. The fire's light illuminates my tears." She took a brief moment to collect herself before adding, matter-of-factly, "Needless to say all this is intercut with the opera we never made it to, already in progress. Puccini's *Tosca*. Have you ever seen it?"

"No."

"It's the opera that's on now."

As if on cue, the passionate soprano belted out tortured Italian verse.

"Wow," he said, not knowing what to say. "You've really thought this out, haven't you?"

"Yes. It's very important to me. What do you think?"

Melodramatic as hell, incredibly over-the-top, there's no way we're going to include this scene in the next two weeks. He briefly considered the possibility of searching for stock footage of a turn-of-the-century carriage at night, maybe from a long-forgotten costume drama, Masterpiece Theatre or something like that. Then maybe he could pick up the rest of the coverage in close ups and ... *fuck, there's no way!*

"Well ..." he said stroking his chin, "that would be a great scene ..." but what he really pondered was *opera house? A dying kid?* Eddie felt a major headache coming on.

"I feel it's critical," and she added with emphasis, "Vital."

"Have you mentioned this to Sam?"

"I've brought it up a number of times, but he puts me off. I figured with your endorsement ..."

Eddie knew Sam would never agree to put up the extra money, but said, "I'll talk to him."

"I think it best if we talk to him together," she suggested.

"Whatever you think."

She smiled. "We're going to make a great movie, you and I."

"I know we are," he said with forced confidence, hoping it was true.

CHAPTER FIFTEEN

"**I**t's a bowhunter's arrowhead, different than the recreational brass rounded-tip arrow the Dillard brothers have," Deputy Martinez explained to Detective Chong.

They were standing beside the gray fabric-covered cubicles inside the Sheriff's office substation. She handed Chong a color Xerox photo of the arrow retrieved from the camera truck and continued, "This broadhead is designed for big-game kill, razor sharp. In bowhunting it's all about bleeding out the game," she said, details she'd learned from speaking with the game warden. "The blades are designed to cut through blood vessels, arteries and vital organs resulting in both internal and external bleeding. The more damage done from the arrow traveling through the body, the quicker oxygen is deprived to the brain. And bowhunters prefer to not have to chase game very far, so this modern design is all about a quick kill." She pointed out the stainless steel tip in the photo. "This is a mechanical broadhead which means it has moving parts, additional blades that pop out upon entering the body to cause maximum damage slicing through flesh."

"Sort of like a hollow-point bullet," Detective Chong said.

"That's right, goes in and expands. And this arrow is the same make and model from the roadside murder." She produced photos of those arrows, the broadhead and shaft tinted reddish-brown from the victim's dried blood. "Different than the arrows we collected out at the Dillard place."

"And this arrow was retrieved where?" he asked.

"Shot at one of the trucks up at the Crescent Movie Ranch this afternoon. There's a crew up there making a movie. Nobody was hurt, thankfully. The truck was parked when it was struck."

"And what type of arrows killed that alpaca?" he asked.

"Those arrows were never collected as evidence."

"Why not?"

Deputy Martinez knew he'd ask so she'd already prepared her response, "It's not department policy to retrieve evidence when animals are killed."

He gave her a nod, said, "So you're saying the Dillard brothers may have had nothing to do with the roadside killing?"

"I know I led everyone to their place, but—"

"Don't regret it," he said.

"Have you found Nick Dillard?"

"Not yet."

"And Jerry? Has he said anything?"

"Didn't make it out of Intensive Care," he said.

A pang of guilt struck Martinez but she tried her best to hide it. Sure, Jerry was manufacturing drugs, and stupid enough to shoot at them, but did he deserve to die? Had Jerry received medical attention sooner maybe he would have lived, but Martinez was aware of the unspoken rule: once a bad guy engages in battle with officers, they've crossed the line. Immediate medical attention becomes less of a priority unless an officer is also injured, and then it becomes top priority. She realized in Jerry's case, the area was not secure for a while and the medics weren't allowed onto the property until the sheriff's deputies determined his brother Nick was not there nor posed a threat.

She thought of the moment when she engaged Jerry to question him for his brother's whereabouts. She could tell he recognized her and she saw the pure hatred in his eyes, as if she'd betrayed him.

Deputy Martinez said to Detective Chong, "My gut tells me the Dillard brothers had nothing to do with the roadside murder and the killer is still out there."

"Keep an eye on this movie crew. Don't hesitate to request additional resources if need be."

"Yes, sir."

"Good work, Martinez."

It had been a long day. Deputy Martinez changed out of her uniform at her locker. She went to the market for groceries and then drove to the apartment complex she called home. She parked her Hyundai under the carport and went to retrieve her son.

The kids of other working parents rarely stayed with Mrs. Gomez past six or seven in the evening, but with her schedule there were many nights when Cesar slept there until she got home. Martinez knocked and the old woman opened the door. Martinez could see her son sitting on the floor watching TV.

"How was he today?" she asked.

"*Siempre es un buen chico*," she said, meaning he was always a good boy. Mrs. Gomez always said that, Martinez came to realize, so it meant nothing.

Cesar got up and ran to her. He clung onto his mother's leg without saying a word. She could feel the warmth of her young son's arms around her thigh and said, "Mommy's home, little one."

Martinez handed her cash, the arrangement they had since Mrs. Gomez was afraid to open a checking account, like many immigrants in her situation, scared that the paper trail could lead to deportation.

Thinking about the arrow incident, she said, "I may be home

late tomorrow too," her son still clinging to her leg.

"Is not a problem," Mrs. Gomez said with a smile.

"No, Mommy. Stay home," Cesar said.

"I wish I could," she said, and thanked the woman before leading her boy off to their one-bedroom apartment.

CHAPTER SIXTEEN

When Eddie got back to the Gold Strike, it seemed like everybody wanted a piece of him. Stuart needed to finalize the child actors with speaking parts, still not cast yet. Wardrobe had questions regarding how to dress tomorrow's extras. The art department wanted to run photos of props by him before they went through the expense of renting from the prop house. He promised everyone he'd be right back and went to his room, but not before getting ice. He poured a pair of airline-sized Ketel Ones—vodka would be least noticeable on his breath when he returned to meet with everyone.

He sat in the padded armchair in his room and sipped, thinking of Sheila. He had not seen her in the lobby. Maybe she was in the bar. He wondered if the connection he'd felt between them had all been in his imagination. That was plausible. Of course, she'd smile and talk to him, he was the director. And wasn't Sheila a budding cinematographer? She was probably angling to one day shoot one of his movies. *Am I a hopeless romantic?* Eddie thought. *Probably.*

But he couldn't deny there was something there. He sensed she felt it too.

Maybe she had that boyfriend back then. A few months ago, he'd seen her out with some guy walking Santa Monica's Third Street Promenade. On one hand, Eddie wanted to kick the guy's ass, but on the other he realized he and Sheila only spent one night together followed up by just a few dates. It's not like they were a couple, so maybe she was with this guy while working on the last movie and then she felt guilty because she'd strayed. She wouldn't admit she'd been unfaithful. She'd come up with an excuse to break it off, like she did. That must be it.

But that didn't stop Eddie from learning the guy's name later that week when he saw him working out in the gym and asked the trainer who he was. Roland. *What kind of name is that?*

From the brief encounters he'd had with Sheila over the last couple of days, it was clear she wasn't interested in him and likely dating this Roland dude. He appeared to be everything Eddie was not, tall and handsome.

So be it. He decided it best to play it cool. If he and Sheila were meant to be with each other then it would happen. If not …

All he knew was he needed to find some kind of love in his life. He was aware the loneliness and depression fueled his drinking. It had become a crutch. He got up and poured the rest of the glass of vodka down the bathroom sink then rinsed the glass.

While brushing his teeth, the incident with the arrow came to mind. He wondered if it was the result of locals not wanting them to film in their backyard. Was someone trying to scare them off? He'd read newspaper articles about hidden marijuana fields up in the mountains protected by armed men. Maybe the movie ranch was close to one of those. He'd ask Stuart if they'd learned anything more.

Eddie went downstairs and after brief meetings with the others, he sat at Stuart's laptop to finalize the child actors, all scheduled for the next weekend. Eddie asked, "That arrow in the camera truck, you learn anything more?"

"No," Stuart said. "I'm thinking maybe someone was hunting

deer. That ranger said those arrows fly four hundred feet per second so the thing could have come from far away."

"Possibly," Eddie said. "But maybe we consider hiring security."

"We have security."

"Where?"

"Staying on set overnight."

Eddie remembered seeing a slovenly, obese rent-a-cop that afternoon, a bottom-of-the-barrel type of guy, the caliber of security guard minimum wage buys. He must be the security Stuart was referring to, the one who'd stay overnight in one of the trailers up on set to keep an eye on things while everyone else slept in the hotel. He didn't think this guy would be enough. "I saw that guy, but he won't be on shift while the rest of us are working. We may need more."

"I have that sheriff's card," Stuart said. "If anything weird happens I'll call her."

"Okay. But I'm thinking maybe it's worth bringing on a few more guys."

"You want to ask Sam for that?" he snapped back. "Maybe shave a day from the schedule to pay for it?"

"I'm just saying—"

"It's not in the budget."

After a pause, Eddie asked, "Then can we dress the guy in wardrobe and work him in as an extra?"

"You know we can't," Stuart said, angered. "And you're well aware of the limited resources we're dealing with." He opened his binder and said, "I accommodated your request by hiring two more extras for tomorrow. I'm working with you, here, okay, but you can't get blood from a stone."

Eddie let it rest. "Okay Stu, no problem. Thanks."

Hushed so the others would not hear, Stuart said, "I don't tell you how to do your job, so please don't tell me how to do mine."

Eddie could see he'd angered him and figured it wasn't worth pursuing. "I'm sorry. We just need to get shooting this damn thing and everything will take care of itself."

"I wish I could be so optimistic."

"Try to relax. Have fun."

"I'll relax when I call wrap on the last day, when I see the taillights of our trucks heading back to LA," Stuart said.

"Seriously?"

"Yes."

"Okay."

Together they made the last of his choices for the child actors and Stuart sent the email to Susan Pike Casting. Stuart closed his laptop and went up to his room, so Eddie drifted into the bar. Sheila was sitting at a table with Giovanni and Luther. The first karaoke song has just begun.

Eddie hated karaoke. He preferred to drink in relative peace with relaxed conversation as opposed to shouting over someone's amateur performance. He felt it would be awkward to join them so instead retreated to his room.

After a nightcap he crawled into bed, Sheila still on his mind.

CHAPTER SEVENTEEN

Sheila got up early, before the crack of dawn, and called Luther to meet her in the lobby. The night before, they'd made plans to be on the first shuttle up the hill. It was a good hour before call time so only a few others were in the van: Stuart, the grip and electric team of John and Paul, and Seth, the hippie production designer she'd barely seen. Sheila always made it a point to get to set early, especially on the first day, even though she was up late singing duets of Neil Diamond's "Sweet Caroline" and Journey's "Don't Stop Believing." Sheila was wide awake, but Luther was gloomy and despondent, probably a little hungover, she figured. There was a morning chill, so Don cranked the heater while they headed up the hill.

About halfway up the road, they came across Diane waiting at the turnout to Tami's cabin. She wore a puffy down vest and was stomping the ground in her Ugg boots while blowing into her hands for warmth. Don slowed to pick her up. Diane thanked him as she boarded and said to all, "It's really cold out there," before she took a seat across the aisle from Sheila. "I saw a baby deer," she shared, glowing, pointing out to the trees.

All business as usual, Stuart said to Diane, "I need Tami camera-ready by ten a.m. latest. Can you make that happen?"

Diane replied, "You've got to talk to Connie and Bonnie, bub. That's their department. I'm just getting the trailer ready."

Sheila thought it funny she so casually called Stuart "bub."

He asked, "I forgot, and you are?"

"Diane."

"That's right, and your responsibility is …?"

"Tami's stylist."

He nodded with a "right" and consulted the call sheet clipped to his binder.

Sheila suspected Diane was more than a stylist—more like Tami's handler. As mad as she was about all the crazy resources that went into Tami's special treatment, she had to admit she was impressed by Diane when she saw her wrestling the barber chair into the trailer. She was obviously strong and not afraid to get her hands dirty. The only other woman on the shuttle, Sheila introduced herself and they made small talk. She was curious and asked, "So, how long have you worked with Tami?"

"Not long. We've done a lot of social media, but this is our first movie together."

That made sense, a twentysomething handling the older actress' social media channels. Someone Tami's age wouldn't know the current trends. Sheila had a few friends back in LA who were relatively young and didn't have any professional experience but had landed lucrative salaried positions in marketing departments because they were up to speed in digital trends.

She and Diane found a common interest in yoga and chatted about what studios they attended. Sheila liked Diane immediately. She had style, and she was cool and cheerful until the shuttle arrived at base camp and Don put an unlit cigarette in his mouth. Diane's mood suddenly changed and she glared at him. As they stood to get off, Diane asked, "You're not going to light that are you?"

"What?" Don said, as if he had no idea what she was talking about.

"You're not going to light that cig after we all get off, are you? Isn't this van nonsmoking? And aren't we in a fire zone?"

Don said nothing, grabbed the pack and gently slid the cigarette back inside.

Diane looked to Stuart for support and asked, "Isn't smoking outside designated areas grounds for dismissal? Didn't you say that back in LA?"

"Don," Stuart said. "Do me a favor, will ya? Don't light up unless you're in the Gold Strike gravel parking lot, like it says on the call sheet."

"Where's the smoking area up here?" he asked, pointing out the window to the cluster of trucks and trailers.

"We haven't figured that out yet."

"Haven't thought of it, have you?" he accused.

"No. Not yet."

"We're going to be up here all day. Will you let me know?"

"Sure," Stuart said. "We'll find a place and put out an ashtray."

"Thanks," Don said, eyeing Diane in the mirror.

They all got off and dispersed. Sheila and Luther were at the camera truck dropping the liftgate when Diane approached. She said, "Did you see that?"

"See what?" Sheila said.

"That driver guy. After we all got off he turned the van around and lit up."

"Really?"

"I saw the flame of his lighter," Diane said with a look of bewilderment. "Amazing. Didn't he listen to us?"

Luther offered, "The dude probably can't help himself. He's hooked."

Sheila said, "He needs to get nicotine gum, or something, that's what I did."

"What a bastard," Diane said before she marched off to open Tami's trailer.

As Sheila watched her go, she noted how quickly Diane had shifted from the elation of seeing a baby deer to pure anger. But Diane had a good point. She was clearly not afraid to speak her mind.

As Luther swung open the cargo door, he asked Sheila, "So what's the first shot?"

CHAPTER EIGHTEEN

At 5:45 a.m. Tom Birch was the first actor in the chair. He'd gone to bed early and gotten a good night's sleep, a strategy to stave off the flu, and it had worked. Although his joints still felt a little achy, he was definitely feeling better.

Karen and Linda, the joined-at-the-hip makeup, hair, and wardrobe team, worked on him in tandem. Karen had applied a light foundation and was powdering his face while Linda steamed the wrinkles out of Tom's suit. A melancholy, old-time blues recording of Bessie Smith filled the trailer. An Italian coffee machine supplied Tom a frothy latte far superior to the common Folgers drip available from the battered, stainless steel urn on the side of the catering wagon. Tom had been on enough productions to know that on day one everyone pulls out the stops. Try getting steamed milk on day ten. *Not a chance.*

"When's Tami due?" he asked.

Although he had spoken to Tami yesterday morning, Tom was a little concerned he had not seen her since arriving, even though he knew she was not staying at the hotel. Tom was working on what to say to her—how to gracefully thank her again for recommending him for the role. On Tami's TV series, Tom had expertly fine-tuned the skill of pouring on the charm, and Tami lapped it up.

"We're not working on Tami." Karen said, matter-of-fact. "She's got her own people."

Tom picked up a bit of resentment in her tone. "Who?" he asked.

"A stylist, Diana or Diane," Karen said. "And Bonnie and Connie."

"They've got their own makeup trailer," Linda added. "The big one."

Tom suppressed a smile.

"Know them?" Karen asked.

"Yes." He was not surprised that Tami brought Connie and Bonnie along. Obviously they *too* knew how to play Tami, how to keep her fragile ego propped up to bank on continuous employment from project to project. "I've worked with Bonnie and Connie before," he confessed, glad to have a couple of familiar faces around. "We were on Tami's series together."

There was a rap on the door.

"Come in," Linda said.

"Stepping," Eddie said before opening the door and climbing the retractable stairs.

"Thank you, Eddie. I haven't heard that term in a while," Karen said.

Eddie entered. "Tom ... Eddie Lyons," he said, extending his hand to shake. "I'm thrilled to have you on board."

"Thank you," Tom said, and got up from the chair. To Karen he asked, "Stepping? What's that mean?"

Karen said, "A term to alert the makeup crew to expect the bump and vibration that comes with stepping onto the trailer, in the event I'm working on you with an eye pencil or something."

"Oh, I get it. Never heard that one." Then to Eddie, Tom said,

"I'm looking forward to working with you." Tom had tried to introduce himself earlier in the hotel lobby, but Eddie was in hushed conversation with some producer type. Tom had sensed it wasn't the best time to make his acquaintance so he'd decided to be patient and wait. He did, however, pick up on a few heated phrases between Eddie and the producer including, "Tami wants what? Boston? An opera?" And then a stifled, "She's fucking nuts." He planned to clue Tami in about this interchange—the disrespectful tone and insolence he'd witnessed, the jabs spoken behind her back. Or maybe he could somehow leverage the information to his advantage. He'd figure it out.

"Excellent work in *The Opposition*," Eddie said. "That's a great movie. I'm a big fan of your work."

"Thank you," Tom said, standing tall. He liked the fact that Eddie mentioned one of his more obscure titles instead of the half-dozen studio pictures Tom had landed small parts in. *The Opposition* was an independent film that premiered at Sundance and got favorable reviews. Tom had a sizable role. It suggested Eddie knew his work and had not simply looked up his credits on the internet.

Even though he knew it was a total long shot, Tom asked Eddie if, by chance, he'd caught him in what Tom considered his best work ever, Shakespeare's *Richard III* on the stage in Cincinnati. He realized the chances Eddie would have seen the play were slim to none, but asked anyway so Eddie would know he was a Shakespearean actor in case he'd missed it on his résumé. Eddie said he'd never been to Ohio. As they made small talk, Tom realized this was the opportune time to ask about something that had been on his mind.

"Take a seat," Tom said, motioning to Karen's stool. "I had a thought I wanted to talk to you about." Tom sat back in his makeup chair. He sensed Eddie hesitate before he pulled the metal stool over and obliged. Tom started in with, "I've been meaning to speak with you about my hat."

"Your hat?"

"Bartholomew's hat," he said, incorporating his character's

name. Tom snapped his fingers. There was no response, so he snapped again.

Linda appeared perplexed for a second but then nodded to herself, spun on her heels, and retrieved the cowboy hat from the rack. She gave it to Tom and he delicately placed it on his head.

"After careful consideration," Tom said, "I've decided that my character should wear this hat. I feel it ... defines him, of sorts." Tom looked into the mirror. He really liked the way it looked. "And Linda agrees," he added. In the mirror he could see Linda and Eddie exchange a look. Linda shook her head no and shrugged.

"Excuse me," Karen said holding up her coffee mug, "but caffeine takes priority at this hour. I'm off for a refill. Anyone?" Nobody acknowledged her so she weaved her way out of the trailer. After the door slammed, there was a brief moment of silence and Tom could tell Eddie was not receptive.

"I don't know," Eddie said, "it seems to me that hat's more of a ranch hand sorta look, not really something the town merchant would wear."

Tom nodded to himself, tilting his head as if taking a moment to actually consider Eddie's opinion. But he'd already made up his mind and said, "I respectfully disagree."

"You don't think it's too informal?" Eddie asked.

"No. I feel it's a stoic choice. Gives my character a certain command of things."

"What do you think, Linda?" Eddie said.

"You guys decide," she said, "I've got other hats if you want to see them."

Tom could see Eddie was asking Linda for a "nay" vote, so he said, "I've seen the other hats and they're not right. This one's perfect."

"Well, if you really, really insist," Eddie said, "but my main concern with you wearing a wide-brimmed hat is your eyes." With that Eddie stood to go.

"My eyes?"

"Yeah," Eddie said, turning back, "we're lighting this film with broad strokes, top light and dramatic. I'm afraid the hat will shadow your eyes in darkness, and I think it's really important we see them. The audience needs to witness your character's transformation because Bartholomew is her trusted ally at first but then later, as you know, betrays her. It would be a shame to miss those subtle moments."

"I hadn't thought of that," Linda said.

Eddie gave her a nod.

Tom considered Eddie's logic. "Why can't you just light me differently?" he asked.

"Because it wouldn't match the rest of the scenes and might feel like you're in a different movie."

In his mind's eye, Tom had already envisioned his character wearing this hat. He hadn't thought about the technical issues. Tom looked in the mirror again. *Damn*, he really liked it, and it did an effective job at masking his baldness, akin to country star Dwight Yoakam.

He didn't want to give in, but Eddie had a good point. *Shit.* "What if I wear it outdoors where there's plenty of light bouncing up into my face, and then I take it off when I step inside?"

"Well … in that case you're playing those interior scenes *hat in hand*. That's a bit submissive, don't you think?"

Tom didn't like the idea of his character fidgeting with the brim of the hat either. *Damn it.* He tried to recall the continuous scenes in the script where he crossed in and out of the general store. A loud knock sounded and the door swung open. Stuart poked his head inside.

"Eddie, there you are," he said. "Excuse me, but we need you on set."

"Right-o," Eddie said, then to Tom. "I don't think that hat is in your best interest, but I like that you're coming to me with ideas. Keep it up. I'm an open door, and all ears."

"Thanks," Tom said, removing the hat, not satisfied. After Eddie stepped out, he looked into the mirror again.

Now that Tom had met the director, he wasn't sure he liked him.

* * *

An hour later, sitting inside his narrow dressing room adjacent to the honey-wagon, Tom was dressed in wardrobe and going over his lines. Connie appeared at the stairs. "Good morning, Tom."

"Connie. Fancy seeing you here."

"Go figure," she said, adjusting her Ray-Ban sunglasses against the glare of the early morning sun. "Tami asked to see you."

Finally, he thought. "How's she doing?"

"Okay, I guess."

As Tom followed Connie to Tami's makeup trailer, he said, "I hear you're all staying in a mountain cabin somewhere around here."

"That's right," she said.

"How is it?"

"Nice, but no TV so I can't watch my shows."

Tom wasn't sure if she meant the TV shows she'd worked on or the shows she regularly viewed. He said, "You're welcome to come down to the hotel. We've got TV there."

"We can't."

"Why not?"

"All that taxidermy shit. Tami would freak."

Tom hadn't thought of that. "So that's why you're not staying at the Gold Strike?"

"We decided it best for Tami not to see that creepy place."

They approached Tami's makeup and hair trailer, and once Tom entered it was clear these digs were far superior to Karen and Linda's workspace. Tami greeted him with a peck on the cheek. Bonnie saluted with "Aloha," then busied herself with an assortment of brushes and powders on the counter. The third member of Tami's vanity team stepped up and introduced herself. "I'm Diane, nice to meet you."

"Nice meeting you as well," he said, considering Diane the most attractive of the three—tall, athletic, and perky. He sat in the chair next to Tami, reached out to lightly touch her arm and said, "We're fortunately again blessed with another opportunity to work together."

"Yes, indeed," Tami said, clenching his hand.

They made small talk about how beautiful the setting was, about a few of the other cast members, and then the subject of the director came up.

"Have you worked with him before?" Tom asked.

"I haven't."

"I understand this project is your labor of love and heard that Chris Sanderson was your first choice."

"He was, but Chris had another commitment. I have confidence we're in good hands with Eddie," she said.

Tom was on the brink of telling her about Eddie's hushed conversation he had overheard but a radio squawked with a voice asking for rehearsal on set.

Connie asked Tom if he could leave so they could begin putting Tami through "the works."

He'd have to tell Tami about the disparaging words exchanged later. Tom made a gracious exit.

Since Tom was scheduled in the very first shot, less than an hour later he was standing on his mark, paper tape on the wood floor. The shot was his reaction from the window of the general store as Tami's stagecoach arrived in town. In the scene he would notice the arrival of Tami, the new schoolteacher, but she would not see him. Tom wished they had already shot Tami's angle so he knew what to react to. There was no actual stagecoach for him, only a C-stand with a piece of yellow tape on it for his eye line. Tom decided it best to play the moment subtle. He trusted the audience would fill in the rest.

After two takes Eddie said, "Great, but can you give me a little more curiosity?"

Tom resented Eddie's direction. *Doesn't he know anything?*

Less than half an hour later, the camera and lights were set for the master shot of the next scene—Tami's character, Elizabeth, as she makes Bartholomew's acquaintance in the general store. Stuart summoned Tami through the radio but was told she was not ready. Tom witnessed a fair amount of anxiety between Eddie and Stuart until finally, twenty minutes later, Tami reported to set, flanked by Connie, Bonnie, and Diane. She wore a striking vintage white-lace dress. Since this scene directly followed the scene introducing Tami's character in the film, he figured the angelic white was by design.

After Stuart and Tami spoke quietly for a moment, she took her place on set.

Eddie introduced Tami to Giovanni. She was clearly charmed by his accent. Giovanni introduced Tami to Sheila. They shook hands. After more introductions Tom and Tami ran a rehearsal. Eddie was satisfied and Stuart called for "last looks," prompting Tami's team to jump in and buzz around her with last-minute adjustments to hair, makeup, and wardrobe.

"Thank you, ladies," Stuart said, "but now we've got to go."

The vanity team paid no attention to Stuart, as if they hadn't heard his order at all. They continued to work on Tami until Stuart drove them off with his clipboard, "Thank you, ladies, thank you very much. Very good, but we've got to shoot now."

"Are you ready?" Eddie calmly asked Tami.

She nodded, yes.

"Roll sound," Stuart barked.

"Speed," a voice sounded from somewhere off-set, in the soundman territory beyond the lights and stands.

Tom saw Sheila hit the switch. They were rolling.

"Scene eleven, take one," Luther said as he held a slate up, clapped it down lightly, then ducked down beside camera.

"Action," Eddie called out.

Busying himself with the ledger on the counter, Tom could hear Tami enter the store. *Take time with this moment,* he reminded himself and waited until she was on her mark before looking up.

"Good morning, madam," he said, removing the prop bifocals perched on his nose, "How can I help you?"

A high-pitched shriek distracted him. It sounded like an animal of some kind. This broke Tom's concentration. He looked to Eddie standing beside camera.

"Cut," Eddie said.

"Sorry," Tom apologized, realizing he should have stayed in the scene and not looked to camera.

But Tami had also broken scene, her hand covering her mouth. "Oh, my God," she said aloud, eyes wide.

"What the hell was that?" Stuart howled over the radio.

A painful whinny followed before a panicked voice came back, "A horse is down! A horse is down!"

CHAPTER NINETEEN

Sheila remained beside camera as the cast and crew rushed outside. This was her conditioned response. Experienced camerapersons are trained to never step away from the lens. Her responsibility was to protect the most delicate and expensive piece of equipment on set. Sheila took pride in the fact that neither lens nor camera had ever been dropped or damaged on her watch. Only after the room had been cleared did she finally lock down the tripod and drape a mini space-blanket over the camera to protect it from dust.

Once finished, Sheila stepped outside to see what was going on. Down the hill, by the horse trailer, she could see Patches hobbling. The horse attempted to steady itself but its front leg was clearly broken—bent back grotesquely, hoof dangling.

Jimmy was trying to pull the animal down by its reins but it reared back, fighting him. Lucky tried to help.

"Oh, my God," Tami said, horrified. She turned away and buried her face in Tom's shoulder.

Jimmy was able to wrestle Patches' head back at an angle and the horse finally relented. It fell to its side with guttural-sounding effort but continued to kick with its hind legs. Eddie, Giovanni, and a couple of grips from the crew were already down there helping Jimmy keep Patches down.

"What happened?" Stuart barked over the radio.

"Don't know," a voice came back.

To the cast and crew standing near, Stuart said, "Okay everyone, take five. Please do not go far. We'll get help for the horse." With that he marched down the hill to join the others.

A worried Diane paced near Sheila, eyes glued on the horse below. She said, "I hear you, I know, I know," loud enough so that Sheila thought she was talking to her.

Sheila asked, "Excuse me, did you say something?"

"No," Diane said, clearly shaken. She gave Sheila a shrug then joined Tami, Bonnie, and Connie. They huddled together and whispered between themselves before moving down the hill. They gave the prone horse a wide berth before ducking into their trailer.

The remaining cast and crew dispersed, and Sheila found herself the last one standing up on set. She felt sorry for the animal, and sick from the incident. She knew it would be considerably longer than five minutes before everyone was back.

Sheila returned to the camera and sat on the seat of the dolly. Instinctively, she pulled out her iPhone to check for messages before remembering there was no cell phone reception. The last of Roland's texts were from last night. She'd caught up and read them all this morning before she got on the shuttle. Who knew if he was still texting her? She wondered how long he'd keep trying to contact her to apologize, and wondered what he'd say. She was curious to know what he was doing at that moment. Is he with Lisa? She thought back to times when the three of them were together, cooking in the kitchen, hanging out, and tried to remember if there were romantic signals between them that she did not pick up on. She wondered who made the first move. She was pretty sure it was Roland, but who knew? He had one hell of a libido.

Alone, sitting next to the camera, she felt incredibly vulnerable. There was nothing in her life now, no family, no boyfriend, and hardly any friends. All she had was her career, and that was going nowhere fast. She thought about moving back to North Carolina but realized there was nothing for her there. Besides, that would be admitting failure. Sheila reminded herself she needed to stay strong. *There's light at the end of the tunnel, I just can't see it yet.*

She hated that there was no cell phone reception because she wanted to finally return Roland's texts to lash out but it would have to wait until the end of the day. He knew her mom had just died. He knew she needed him now more than ever. How could he be so cold?

Why does heartbreak have to hurt so much?

Alone, Sheila allowed tears to flow. She couldn't let anyone from the crew see her, but there wasn't anyone around and nobody was coming back anytime soon. This was a safe place. Nobody would ever know. It reminded her of that movie *Broadcast News* when Holly Hunter snuck private moments to cry all by herself, then got back to her frantic life. Sheila let herself weep, got it out of her system, and afterward felt better.

Over an hour later, Stuart was able to assemble everyone except Tami back to set. Sheila learned that Patches had gotten spooked and somehow broke his leg while coming out of the horse trailer. Stuart made an announcement that a veterinarian was tending to the animal and that, "everything was going to be fine."

Sheila was in earshot when Eddie pulled Stuart aside. "Don't sugarcoat it," Eddie said. "They're going to have to put the horse down."

"How do you know?"

"I've seen plenty of horses break down. With the front leg like that ..." Eddie said, shaking his head.

"What makes you the expert?" Stuart said, annoyance in his tone.

"I've been to the track enough to know when a horse can be

saved and when it needs to be euthanized."

"But it's not a racehorse. It doesn't need to run."

"Doesn't matter. The animal would go crazy from the pain, and a host of other problems would likely follow."

"Like what?" Stuart asked.

"Infection. I'm not an expert, but if the vet decides to put it down … it's the right thing to do."

"So killing the horse is the right thing?" Stuart said, cynical.

"If you don't believe me, ask the vet."

Twenty minutes later Tami still had not reported to set. After much conversing on the radio, Sam Carver arrived and held a brief conference with Eddie, Giovanni, and Stuart. Then Stuart announced to all that Tami would not be working for the rest of the day. Sheila could see Eddie took this hard.

The remainder of the workday was spent shooting a handful of short scenes and pieces of scenes in and around the Western town. Since Jimmy and Lucky were tied up with Patches, no horses were available for the background. Giovanni's solution was to shoot with long lenses so the audience wouldn't miss them. Wide lenses show off more of the location, but a long lens features the subjects up close while the background falls out of focus. Sheila was tasked with keeping focus, never easy using long lenses. She hoped she'd nailed it but wasn't sure.

To Stuart's dismay, Eddie was right. Sheila watched the veterinarian, a middle-aged woman dressed in a polo shirt and khakis, pull out an oversized hypodermic needle from a leather pouch and approach the horse. After a few minutes, it stopped breathing and she covered the carcass with a tarp.

Jimmy the wrangler stood aside, devastated.

Sheila felt incredibly sad. There had been so much death in her life, first her mother, and now this. Lunch was served, but she didn't feel like eating.

They went back to work and later that afternoon an old black truck arrived. Men in jumpsuits piled out. Sheila was expecting a large animal ambulance of some kind, something white and official looking. Instead a sign on the side of the greasy truck read Tri-County Rendering and, upon closer inspection, in smaller letters, By-Product Processing. The men hooked the carcass to a winch. It slowly pulled the limp horse through the dust, up a ramp, and into the truck. Black diesel smoke spewed from the truck's exhaust before it drove away.

With the grisly image of the lifeless horse being dragged through the dirt ingrained in her brain, Sheila had a hard time concentrating. She blew a shot and they had to reset to do another take, her fault. Sheila felt horrible and apologized. It seemed everybody was off their game.

At wrap, Sam returned and summoned Eddie, Giovanni, and Stuart for another meeting. Sheila could sense thick tension as they all piled into Don's van for the drive down the hill. Then, with help from Luther, she put everything away, locked the camera truck, and caught the shuttle back to the Gold Strike.

The buffet dinner was a somber affair. Jimmy had clearly been drinking. He grew emotional as he explained what had happened. "Patches' hoof got caught in the space between the trailer and the ramp," he said, "then she panicked, didn't understand."

He clearly loved the horse. Sheila felt sorry for him.

After dinner, most moved to the hotel bar or sat around the lobby with their noses in cell phones or laptops, but Sheila went to her room and took a hot shower. Afterward, wrapped in a Gold Strike terry-cloth robe, she finally gave in. It was time to return Roland's call.

"Hey," she said, cautious.

"Did you get my voice mails and texts?"

"Yes."

"Why didn't you respond?"

She said nothing.

"Sheila … I'm sorry. Let me expl—"

"How could you?"

"I don't know. It just happened. I don't love Lisa, I love you."

"Bullshit!" she said. "If you loved me you wouldn't be fucking her."

There was a pause before he said, "It's not what you think."

"What should I think, Roland? She's my roommate."

"I don't know."

"How long has this been going on?"

"When you were in North Carolina I ran into her one night."

"Where?"

"The Third Street Promenade."

"In a bar?"

"Misfit. It was random. I'd forgotten my leather jacket at your place so we went back to get it. It just sort of happened," he said.

"You made it happen."

He said nothing.

"And you kept going back," she accused.

"Her idea."

"You agreed."

More silence.

"How many times?"

"I don't know. I'm sorry."

"Tell me how many more times."

"Does it matter?"

"I hate you," she said and hung up on him. He called back but she didn't answer, put her phone on silent. She thought about calling Lisa and screaming at the bitch, asking her why she stabbed her in the back, but decided it was best not to engage. *Fuck her.*

She turned on the TV to take her mind off it all and eventually fell asleep.

In her dream she was sitting in the makeup trailer and looking at herself in the mirror. She felt an increasing tightness in her chest, couldn't breathe, and the color of her skin was rapidly changing. It was

just like what she'd witnessed when her mother's life slipped away—
her skin transforming from living flesh-tone to a lifeless, ashen gray.

She awoke and for a moment didn't know where she was, then
remembered that she was in a hotel room, on a shoot. She went into
the bathroom and turned on the light. In the mirror she could see
she wasn't dying, at least not tonight, but she thought she looked old
and haggard. *No wonder why he left me. Lisa is prettier than me.* She
checked her phone. There were texts, ones he'd sent after she'd hung
up—"Call me, I'm sorry"—plus a voice mail. She couldn't forgive
him. It was over, and she knew it. Why did it have to hurt so much?

Sheila set the alarm on her phone, pulled down the covers,
and crawled into bed. *Onward*, she willed herself. *No turning back.*
She imagined what Roland was doing, whether he'd go to Lisa and
spend the night. Would they talk about her? Probably. She tried to
force herself to think of something else. She wondered where those
men had taken the dead horse.

CHAPTER TWENTY

Eddie, after the disastrous first day, was focused on one thing only—getting his drink on. But he knew he had business to attend to first. Immediately after wrap he'd joined Stuart, Giovanni, and Sam for an emergency production meeting. In Carver's hotel suite, Sam dropped the bomb and explained, "Tami's agent doesn't think she can work tomorrow." Sam then asked Stuart to see if it was possible to "adjust the schedule in the event Tami, in her fragile state of mind," as he facetiously phrased it, "needs more than a day to collect herself."

"The trouble is," Stuart said, "Tami's in almost every scene. If she doesn't work tomorrow, or the next day, we're boned."

"Boned?" Sam questioned.

"It wouldn't be good."

The urge for a drink was so strong and Eddie had a hard time concentrating. He envisioned the mini vodka bottles waiting in the drawer of his room, calling his name. No, maybe he'd go for the single malt scotch. The "brown" would certainly put him in the right place, the warm and safe environment he yearned for.

Sam said, "Eddie, you've got to talk to Tami. Make her promise to work tomorrow. Can you do that?"

"Now?"

"Yes, go see her."

The brown would have to wait.

* * *

As Diane answered the door, Eddie could see she'd been crying, eyes red, mascara slightly smeared. "Hey, Diane. You all right?"

She gave him a nod but he could tell she was covering up.

"Tami here?" he asked.

"Come in." She led him through the foyer and said, "That was so cruel."

"A horrible accident," Eddie said.

"That poor horse's leg bent back like that," Diane said. "And then to kill ... they didn't have to do that," she said with resentment, "they could have saved her. You could have insisted. You're the director."

Eddie said nothing.

They entered the living room. Tami was on the phone.

"Can I get you anything to drink?" Connie asked.

"No, thank you," Eddie said, figuring it would be bad form to ask for what he really wanted.

"My director's here," Tami said into the phone, "Let me call you back." She hung up. Clearly flustered, the receiver fell out of the cradle and she fumbled with it before placing it back on its stand. "We're all so shaken," she said. "That poor horse."

"Tragic," Eddie said. "Are you all right?"

"Hardly."

He sat next to her on the couch.

"Why did they have to kill her?" Diane asked.

"That was more than just a fracture, it was a snapped leg," he explained. "The horse would never be able to stand again. The wound would likely become infected and Patches would suffer a painful, horrible death. As majestic and powerful as horses are with all that muscle, they are also quite delicate."

"You know a lot about them?" Diane asked cynically.

"Some. I know from horse racing," he said.

"Horse racing?" she questioned with a tone of disdain.

"I've been to the track a few times. Some of my colleagues have owned racehorses and I know a few trainers."

Disapprovingly, Diane snorted and crossed her arms.

"We're all so crushed," Tami said. "That was my agent, Bernie, on the phone. We've been discussing it," she said, her eyes becoming glassy, "and I don't know if I can …"

"Tami, it's crucial that we press on. We can't let this unfortunate incident stop us from making your wonderful movie."

"I'm an emotional wreck," she said, tears welling.

"I understand, but I sense you're also very strong."

"I'm not that strong. I'm extremely sensitive, especially when it comes to animals."

"If this were the Old West, what would your character do?"

Tami paused to consider.

"She wouldn't give up," Eddie continued. "She'd dust herself off and press on."

"Have you spoken to Sam about our Boston scene, and how important that is to me?"

He knew he couldn't be honest at that moment. Eddie said, "Yes, and we're looking into how we can include it in our schedule. It will have to be shot back in town. Universal has a brownstone street on their backlot that will pass for old Boston. I'm thinking we shoot there one night." Eddie knew Sam had no intention of including that scene, but this was not the time to deliver the bad news.

"Universal?" she said, hopeful.

"Yes."

Tami nodded and looked around to the others for support. They all shared silent nods before Tami dropped her head, rubbed her temples, and only after a deep, dramatic sigh announced, "You're right. We *shall* press on."

"It's the right thing to do," Eddie said.

"I want to dedicate the film to that pony."

"Excuse me?"

"Like they do for cast and crew that pass away during a production, you know, you've seen it, a title card at the end. The very first card before the final credits roll, and then maybe with a picture of Patches. Can we do that? And plug my nonprofit?"

"I think it's a wonderful idea," said Eddie. Now he *really* needed a drink.

"If you can promise me that ..."

Eddie stood. He could not promise anything but instead bellowed, "A horse! A horse! My kingdom for a horse," for Tami's benefit.

Tami applauded and said, "Yes, yes. Shakespeare."

"Excuse me, but I have much to do tonight. Can I expect to see you at call time?" he asked Tami, then turned to the others, "All of you?"

The women looked to Tami.

She gave them a nod. "We'll be there," Tami said. "With bells on."

* * *

"Thank God," Sam said, relieved when Eddie returned with the good news. "Let's celebrate." He grabbed the room service menu. "I'll have them bring up a bottle of champagne."

Eddie's mind was already set on scotch, not wimpy-ass champagne. "I have an idea," he suggested, "I've got a bottle of single malt in my room. What do you say I get that and save you the expense of room service?"

"It's no big deal."

"Sure, but we deserve a proper dram, sir. It's what men drink. Scotch whiskey. And the way they mark up room service around here …" Eddie said, having a pretty good idea Sam would choose the less expensive option.

"That's why I like you, Eddie. Not only can you calm the nerves of our crazy actress but you're always thinking about how to save the production a buck."

"My aesthetic is all about economy."

"Get the whiskey."

By the time Eddie retrieved the bottle and returned to Sam's suite, Mike had brought up paper plates of spaghetti from the buffet and filled the ice bucket. Eddie poured for Sam, himself, and Mike. With things back on track, Eddie could finally relax. He took a seat in the armchair and sipped. They ate pasta and over-buttered garlic bread and washed it down with twelve-year-old scotch.

After receiving a text message on his phone, Mike excused himself, "I'll be downstairs if you need me."

"His girlfriend," Sam said after Mike was gone. "To be in our early twenties again, my friend, chasing tail … those were the days."

Eddie remembered seeing Sam's sultry brunette receptionist in the hotel lobby on the coach snuggled close to Mike and figured she was his girlfriend. "He's a good kid," Eddie said.

"Yeah, but he's still got a lot to learn."

They poured another and Eddie told him about Tami's request to dedicate the film to the dead horse.

"She is *truly* insane," Sam said, scratching the back of his head.

"I think we should play it like we plan on shooting this Boston scene, as a pickup back in town after principal photography, just to appease her for now."

Sam shook his head and said, "It's not in the budget, and I can't ask for more."

Eddie remembered the cash payment he delivered to the casting director, then asked, "Where's the money coming from, anyway?"

Sam got up and plopped fresh ice cubes into his glass. "This goes no further, understand?"

"Of course."

"Between you and me, the investors are a pair of guys I met when I was at the US Open in New York. They had box seats next to me in Arthur Ashe Stadium and we immediately hit it off. When they learned what I did for a living, they sparked to the idea of investing in Hollywood."

"What kind of business are they in?"

"Let's just say they're in the hospitality business."

"Mob?"

"I can't say for sure, but I have suspicions."

"Why's that?"

"By the way they handled themselves, and the questions they asked."

"Money laundering?" Eddie asked him, hushed even though they were alone in the room.

"Likely. I've never seen so much cash in my life, but that's how they prefer to do business. You've got to keep this under wraps. Nobody knows except you. Not even Mike."

"I promise."

"You'll meet them tomorrow. They're coming by the set, the two brothers. They're out here looking at some commercial property in Orange County."

"When?"

"Don't know. They're driving up from Newport Beach, so whenever they get here. You've got to help me give them the ole dog and pony show, then we'll send them on their way."

"It's not the first time I've had investors come around," Eddie said to assure Sam he was fine with it. "I'll make sure they feel welcome."

"If we can put this one in the can without too many surprises they'll do all right by their investment, once I get the license fee from the network and shore up a home video deal. Then eventually, say a year from now, if I'm lucky, I'll see my end from foreign sales. I suspect Tami's name still has value overseas. And Westerns are back in style, so ..."

"And what if you're not lucky?"

"Then I'm broke."

"Wow," Eddie said. "Really?"

Sam nodded, sipped.

"How do you do it?" Eddie asked.

"Do what?"

"Take such risks?"

"It's like this," Sam explained, "you've got to charge the net. You can't wait at the baseline and play it safe, not if you're going to win. It's all about timing, and angles," Sam swung his wrist as if he held a tennis racket. "In life, it's about winning ... game, set, and match."

"Without risk there's no gain," Eddie said.

"That's right, my friend. Besides, I've got no choice in the matter. My ex-wives ... they'll skin me alive if they don't get their alimony checks. It's like they're in collusion. Greedy bitches."

Eddie laughed and said, "No love lost there."

"*Love* means nothing in tennis," Sam said, matter-of-fact.

Eddie toasted him and sipped his scotch.

CHAPTER
TWENTY-ONE

Tom stood in the general store the following morning waiting to do his scene.

Tami was not on set yet, and he had a pretty good idea why. He suspected the conversation they had earlier that morning had started something. At call time, Tom had visited Tami's trailer to enlist her support for the cowboy hat Eddie wouldn't allow him to wear. He'd thought long and hard about it while looking into the mirror in his hotel room that morning. He didn't care if his face was in shadow in some of the scenes. It would serve to make Bartholomew more mysterious. That could be a good thing. His intention was to get Tami to veto Eddie's decision so he'd get his way. And besides, the director of photography could make a little compromise in the way he lit the film. Add another lamp, what's the big deal? He put the hat on to show her but Tami wasn't sure, so she deferred to Diane, her stylist. When Diane shot it down, Tom was disappointed but tried his best not to show it. *What does she know?*

They invited him to stay for a cup of chamomile tea, and, warming his hands around the cup, Tom enlightened Tami to the conversation he'd overheard between Eddie and Sam the other day. In a lowered voice, but not so low that Bonnie, Connie, and Diane couldn't hear, he said it was his impression that Eddie and Sam were "disrespectful." He could see Tami was growing indignant and added, "It was clear to me they have no intention of granting your wish, whatever it is."

This infuriated Tami.

Now the entire cast, crew, and background artists waited as Eddie, Sam, and Tami held another "emergency meeting" in her trailer. Tom figured he'd be getting his overtime. *Nice.*

Meanwhile, Giovanni used the extra time to set additional backlight. The art department fussed with set dressing. Connie, Bonnie, and Diane, not in the closed-door meeting, tied up the grips, requesting they build a shaded space for Tami's chair near the set.

Stuart spent the entire time on his radio trying to track down Jimmy the wrangler. Jimmy was seen the night before in the hotel bar and had not reported at call time. Lucky, the assistant wrangler, hadn't seen him either and now was working single-handed.

While he was waiting, Tom checked out the assistant camera chick. He thought she had a sexy tomboy thing working in her favor and liked the snug fit of her fleece top. He snuck looks from time to time, and was intrigued by the way her pullover hugged the curvature of her breasts. His imagination got the best of him.

"How far are we behind schedule, anyway?" Tom asked, pretending he was concerned.

Sheila pulled a folded piece of paper from the back pocket of her black jeans, consulted it and said, "According to the call sheet, about a half day unless they decide to cut a few scenes."

Tom knew that wasn't going to happen. Tami's character was in most of the scenes and she'd insist they all be included. "Tom," he said, introducing himself with his hand out.

"Sheila," she said, offering hers.

"Sheila? Like from that Buddy Holly song?" he said.

"Tommy Roe song, actually, but it sounds like a Buddy Holly tune. A lot of people mistake it."

"I remember … something about a ponytail? Goes *My Little Sheila.*"

"That's the one," she said with an exhale. "A one-hit wonder."

"Don't the Australians—"

"Yeah, yeah. *Sheila* is slang for *girl* down under. My father was from Melbourne. Apparently he had a sense of humor."

"Apparently?"

"Never knew him."

Daddy issues. Tom had slept with enough women from fractured homes to see the pattern. He entertained a brief fantasy that she'd be subservient in the bedroom before he strategized how to best compliment her and keep the conversation going. He caught her eye and said, "I like the name Sheila. It's cool and unique. Very hip."

"Thanks," she said and turned away, busying herself with the camera.

Tom figured he'd planted the seed and would work on her later.

Moments later he noticed a black Land Rover pull into base camp. Two men in their fifties emerged, both wearing suits. They appeared out of place among the pine trees, more fitting for the boardroom or Fifth Avenue. Sam emerged from Tami's trailer and greeted them. They chatted for a moment and Sam led them up to set.

Sam was giving them a tour, pointing out the sets, equipment, and props. They stood at the perimeter nodding their heads and Stuart joined them. Both men were overly tan and wore fine leather loafers which Tom considered impractical footwear for the rugged mountain terrain. Sam led them closer and made introductions to Giovanni. Tom was next.

"Tom, meet our executive producer team, Anton and Fritz."

Tom offered his hand, "Nice to meet you." From their accents,

Tom could tell they were either Russian or from somewhere in Eastern Europe. A little rough around the edges, Tom assumed they were new money.

Sam informed, "Tom plays Bartholomew, the proprietor of the general store," motioning to the set. "He's the bad guy."

"Not bad … simply misunderstood," Tom said, stoic, making a joke.

The humor went over their heads. Fritz instead said to Tom, "I've seen you in movies, no?"

"Yes," he said, liking that he had been recognized by a stranger. Before he could say anything more, the two men exchanged words in some sort of Slavic-sounding language.

"Let me introduce you to our star, Tami," Sam said before he led them down to base camp.

Tom figured by the way they were dressed and the way Sam treated them they were the film's financiers. *Russians investing in Hollywood?* he thought. *Isn't it supposed to be the Chinese these days?* To Tom, they certainly looked like they could afford the overtime he planned to milk.

All this waiting around … the longer the better.

After Sam knocked on the door of Tami's trailer, the men entered. Eddie emerged and returned to set. He and Stuart spoke aside in hushed tones but Tom overheard that Tami was coming. Things appeared to be back on track.

Diane broke the silence with, "What the fuck?!"

Tom turned to see her holding a cigarette butt. She displayed it for all to see with, "Whose is this?"

Nobody responded.

Diane turned to Stuart and said, "Who are you going to fire for smoking up here, bub? Or was all that a bunch of bull?"

Put on the spot, Stuart asked all assembled, "Okay, who was smoking up here on set?" Silence followed so he continued, "Let me make this clear. If you are caught smoking anywhere outside of the designated areas then pack your bags. No exceptions." To Diane, motioning to the cigarette butt, Stuart said, "Give me that."

"Why?"

"I'll compare it to the brand people smoke."

She sniffed it. "Whose? Don's?"

"Maybe it's not from us."

She handed it over, said, "You do that, Sherlock Holmes."

"Can you check on Tami please? We're falling behind schedule."

Diane did not budge.

"Here she comes," Eddie said.

Sam and the two financiers escorted Tami up to set. Tami gave Tom a knowing nod. Without asking, he knew she'd gotten her way. Hopefully, whatever it was, it all penciled out in his favor. After final touches from hair and makeup, Tami was ready and the scene got underway.

Tami had fire in her, he could see. Tom played off her vibrant energy.

After the scene in the general store was shot, with much time spent on Tami's close-up, they moved on to complete the scene when Tami's character arrives by stagecoach, the scene that had been partially shot the day before.

The transportation guys brought up the vintage wagon. Lucky, with the help of a production assistant who had some riding experience, hooked two horses to the carriage. Tom could see Lucky was dressed in wardrobe and learned he would be the driver of the coach. Because the tattoos up his neck were clearly visible, the frazzled wardrobe girls had to scramble for a solution. Finally, they came up with a kerchief to tie around his neck.

Potbellied Don was also in costume and would, apparently, ride shotgun. Tom thought they both looked ridiculous but figured it made sense. You wouldn't expect a background extra to know how to drive a stagecoach. They cleared a path for the wagon to loop around and reset for multiple takes.

When the camera was ready, Tom was instructed to stand on his mark, by a sandbag set on the splintered planks of the wooden sidewalk. The angle would tie him into an over-the-shoulder shot. He could see Sam standing next to the financiers watching it all unfold. They seemed especially intrigued by the stagecoach and horses.

Stuart called for Tami. Her handlers were careful to not allow the white lace of her dress to drag in the dirt. Diane was especially attentive, making last-minute adjustments, and Tom could see Tami grow impatient with her fidgeting. "Enough!" Tami snapped, short-tempered. Tom saw that Diane was hurt. She stayed back and let the others do the final primping.

The grips, Paul and John, placed apple boxes as temporary steps so Tami could climb into the coach. After brief instructions from Eddie, Stuart said, "People, we have to go," clearly trying to move it all along. Stuart opened the stagecoach door for her. Tami climbed the boxes and slipped inside.

There was a blood-curdling scream.

Tami jumped out in a panic. The actress stumbled face-first into the dirt, her pure white dress smeared in blood. "There's a man in there!" she screeched.

Tom was closest. He jumped in to help Tami to her feet and saw Jimmy, the wrangler who cared for the horses, lying on the stagecoach floor. An arrow stuck out of his bloody, mangled eye.

CHAPTER
TWENTY-TWO

Sheila couldn't take her eyes off Jimmy. She thought it was so strange the arrow pierced the center of his hand, as if it was a stigmata wound, then continued into his eye. The shaft of the arrow propped his hand up as if the bloody corpse was waving to her. It gave her the chills.

As grotesque as it was, she couldn't look away.

Stuart shouted, "Okay, people, don't panic! Please wait down at base camp until further notice!" More than half the cast and crew had already dispersed, but Sheila, Luther, and Giovanni stood near the camera.

"Let's break everything down and pack up," Sheila suggested.

"Not yet," Giovanni said.

"Why not?"

"Wrap is not my call."

"I'm not saying we wrap," Sheila said. "I say we break the camera, put the lenses away."

"I'll let you know. Do nothing."

Sheila could tell Giovanni was shaken.

Luther, on the other hand, was enraged. "Somebody killed that dude!" he growled, stating the obvious.

"Jimmy's hand up like that, pierced by the arrow," Sheila said, "it's so weird."

"Maybe he was trying to pull it out," Giovanni ventured.

Sheila said, "It's as if the arrow went through his hand first then continued into his face."

The three shared a look.

"It's like ..." she continued, "Jimmy saw it coming. He was holding up his hand in defense."

"Like this?" Giovanni demonstrated with his left hand out in front of him.

"He was pleading for his life," Sheila pointed out.

"Let's get the fuck out of here," Luther said, looking out to the trees.

They headed down the hill, reached base camp and joined the others. Sam was clearly distraught. He and the Russians spoke among themselves before all three of them climbed into the Land Rover and sped away.

Luther began telling those assembled about how an arrow had pierced the camera truck the day before. This prompted a nervous murmur from the crew and suspicious looks out to the trees. Many took cover in the crevices the trucks and trailers offered. Tami and her team had found shelter inside her custom trailer but refused to open the door.

Deputy Sondra Martinez soon arrived, her squad car sliding to a stop in a plume of dust far worse than Luther's from the other day. Sheila couldn't believe she was stupid enough not to shut the doors of the camera truck, but it was understandable considering the circumstances.

Deputy Martinez got out and Sheila jumped down from the tailgate to direct her. "Up there," Sheila said, pointing to the stage-coach up the hill.

Martinez marched up to join Eddie, Stuart, and Lucky standing near the stagecoach. Sheila watched Martinez reach inside and assumed she must be checking Jimmy's pulse. Next she took out an iPhone and photographed the body, occasionally batting flies away.

Tami emerged from her trailer, cleaned up and out of the bloodied wardrobe. She and her entourage were just in time as Don drove over in the passenger van. Diane opened the door and they were the first to climb in.

Deputy Martinez saw this and came running down. "Hold up," she shouted. Eddie, Stuart, and Lucky followed. "Everybody stays here. Out! Out of the van!" barked the deputy.

"I'm diabetic, I need my insulin," Tami pleaded from inside the van.

"I said get out," the deputy ordered.

Diane stepped out and came to Tami's defense, "But you don't understand, she's—"

"Nobody goes anywhere until I say so! Out of the van, ladies, now."

Sheila could see Tami didn't like being told what to do as the actress and her entourage reluctantly complied. The deputy turned to the cast and crew and asked, "Does anyone have gum, candy, or something we can give her?"

Paul produced beef jerky from his pocket, "I've got buffalo jerky."

"I'll be fine," Tami said meekly.

"You sure? I've got plenty," offered Paul, taking a bite himself.

"I'll manage, thank you."

"There are Red Vines on the craft service table," Stuart announced, snapping his fingers as if to prompt someone, anyone other than himself, to immediately run for them. Nobody did.

"I don't eat licorice. I'll be fine," Tami said.

"You've got to eat something," Deputy Martinez demanded. "I can't have a diabetic seizure complicating things."

"I assure you, I'll be fine, thank you," Tami said.

"If you get light-headed you've got to let me know."

Tami nodded moments before the squalid plastic tub of Red Vines was brought to her. The container of red twists was as common as bottled water and found on every craft service table. When Sheila had first started working on movies she'd often indulge in a few strands from time to time but stopped once she came to the realization that practically everybody from the crew sifts their grubby hands through that plastic container—grips, electrics, extras, production assistants—probably not the cleanest dispenser on earth.

"Come on," Deputy Martinez urged.

Tami hesitated at first, but then reached in and dug out a flimsy strand. She held it up for the officer's benefit.

Martinez waited.

Tami bit and chewed.

Satisfied, Deputy Martinez turned to all and asked, "Who was in the vehicle I passed on the way up here?"

Stuart said, "That was our executive producer and some of our financiers."

"Why were they leaving the scene of a crime?"

Stuart didn't have an answer so simply shrugged.

"I need them to come back, and I need their contact info," she said.

Stuart nodded. "Okay."

"Did anyone see what happened?"

Collective silence followed.

"Anything out of the ordinary? Anything suspicious?" Martinez pressed.

More silence.

"Who was the last to see the victim?" the officer asked, thumbing back over her shoulder.

Sheila remembered the last time she saw Jimmy was at dinner the night before. Before then she remembered him pacing like a caged animal just before the veterinarian put Patches down.

"His name is Jimmy," Lucky informed.

"Thank you. Who was the last to see Jimmy?"

Paul raised his hand, jerky still in his mouth, and said, "I saw him in the bar last night before I crashed."

"What bar?" she asked.

"The Gold Strike down the hill," Stuart explained. "We're all staying there."

"Right." She pulled out her notepad, "What time?"

"Just past midnight or so," Paul said. "After last call."

She jotted that down. "And you are …?"

"Paul Reynolds. Chief electrician."

"Did anybody see Jimmy this morning?" she asked.

Many of the crew looked to Lucky who shrugged and said, "I knocked on his room early this morning but he didn't answer."

"And when was that?" Martinez asked.

"Five-thirty or so," Lucky said. "It was still dark."

Sheila could see Deputy Martinez was trying to determine an approximate time of death.

"Understand this is a crime scene," Deputy Martinez announced. "I'll need everyone to be patient. Nobody goes anywhere, is that understood? Please be patient."

As horrible as the situation was, Sheila liked the way the deputy remained calm and in control.

"Look, deer!" Connie shouted, pointing up the hill.

Sheila turned to see a half-dozen deer running across the Western town above them. Prancing, darting, the grace of the animals took her breath away.

"Oh, they're beautiful," Tami exclaimed.

But Sheila's impression was that these deer were not necessarily at peace. The animals appeared in full flight, running from something. They leaped around the sets and darted for cover into the trees and thick brush. The magnificent animals were gone as fast as they came.

Stuart asked the deputy, "Arrows … do you think somebody is trying to hunt deer?"

"Could be," she said.

"*Merda*," Giovanni barked, eyeing the treetops adjacent to everyone. Sheila followed his gaze to see what he was referring to.

Flames were licking the tops of the pines.

"Fire!" someone shouted.

"Holy shit," Tom said.

"Game changer," Martinez said. "Listen up! I'll need everyone to evacuate in an orderly fashion," she announced. "The Gold Strike … we'll all calmly make our way down and convene there. Is that understood?"

Sheila watched the flames in awe. She wondered how much time it would take before the fire engulfed the entire bank of trees.

"Don will shuttle everyone down," Stuart said, "so line up," and then to Don, Stuart asked, "Where's the stakebed truck?"

"Out picking up supplies," he said in a worried tone. "All we have is the van."

"Then you'll have to make a couple of trips," Eddie said.

Don nodded. "Copy that."

"It's your fault!" an enraged Diane screamed at Don. "What'd you do, flick your cigarette butt out the window?"

"Don't look at me," he replied.

"Calm and orderly, is that understood?" the Deputy instructed. "Please do not panic. There's plenty of time to evacuate. We'll all meet down the hill and assess the situation."

But most did panic.

There was a sudden rush for the van.

Tami was the first to jump in, followed by Connie, Bonnie, and Diane, still seething and cursing under her breath. Tom climbed in next, but Stuart shouted, "Women first!" so he reluctantly gave up his seat. As Tom climbed out of the van, Sheila heard Tom mutter, "What is this, the *Titanic*?"

Sheila's first instinct was to run up to the set and grab the camera and lenses. She watched as the deputy went to her squad car and got on the radio. Martinez pulled an electronic device off the dashboard and into the radio announced "latitude" followed by a list of numbers. Sheila recognized the spoken code as GPS coordinates.

Sheila turned to Giovanni. "I'm going for the camera," she said. She wished they'd broken the camera apart earlier, when she suggested.

"Don't worry about it, everything's insured," he said.

"But the media cards. It's got everything we've shot so far."

Giovanni said nothing. He turned to study the smoke coming from the trees. "I'll drive the camera truck," he offered.

Paul said, "We can take a handful down in the grip truck."

"Great. Do that."

Karen and Linda, the original hair and makeup team, were closest in proximity, so they followed Paul to the grip truck. After the van was stuffed with its first load of passengers, the vehicle took off. Next the grip truck set out. Sheila could see, other than the deputy, she was the only woman left.

Giovanni said, "Okay, let's get those cards."

With that she, Giovanni, and Luther climbed the hill.

Up on set, Lucky was freeing the horses from the stagecoach. He smacked them on the rear with a hearty "Git!" but the animals would not scatter.

Sheila couldn't help but gaze once again at Jimmy's dead body while pulling the camera apart. She wondered if the fire would reach the stagecoach and if Jimmy's corpse would be charred beyond recognition. The camera equipment went into cases and they were all snapped shut. Then she, Luther, and Giovanni carried it all downhill.

Lugging cases, Sheila watched the burning trees. Smoke billowed into the sky, as if in slow motion. It seemed so surreal.

The tailgate down, they were able to load the cases quickly. Sheila stood on the liftgate and watched the smoke, wondering how long it would take for the fire to spread. It seemed like an eternity, but the passenger van finally arrived to shuttle down the second load. Sheila heard Eddie and Stuart arguing below. Eddie said, "I'm the captain of this ship, so I'll be the last to get on that shuttle."

"We don't need a martyr, Eddie, we need a director," Stuart argued.

"After I make sure everyone's safe," Eddie countered.

"That's my responsibility."

"Ours together."

The discussion was cut short when Deputy Martinez joined them. "Assistant Manager," she addressed Stuart. "I need you to get on this shuttle. Make sure nobody leaves the Gold Strike. Can you do that for me?"

Stuart suggested, "I think it's best that I—"

"I need you to insure that nobody jumps in their cars and drives home, is that clear? Have your producer and whoever else was in that Land Rover meet us there too. We need everyone together. An officer will join you, but he doesn't know anyone from the cast and crew. You do. You have that list. I'll be down there shortly. Can I count on you?"

"Sure. What about—?"

"Firefighters are on their way."

"Okay."

Like sardines, the next group of passengers was packed into the van. Stuart managed to wriggle himself in, a tight squeeze. "I'll see you down there," he said to Eddie before the sliding door closed and the van departed.

Sheila jumped off the tailgate and said, "We're good to go." The smoke was beginning to make her eyes water.

Luther pushed the button of the lift. The electrical engine whirred but the mechanical gate would not engage. "Oh, shit," Luther said. He pushed the button again and again without luck.

Giovanni saw this and jumped into the cab of the camera truck. Sheila could see him pull keys from the visor and attempt to start the engine. No luck there, this truck's battery was clearly dead.

"Bastards!" Giovanni cursed and jumped out.

Sheila could see he was on the verge of one of his mini tantrums. She intercepted with, "Giovanni, it's fine, we'll go down in the shuttle."

"Always shitty trucks! No prime lenses! No time to make anything good … I am *so* sick of these fucking TV movies," he barked before reverting to his native language, "*Porco Giuda!*"

"Giovanni," Sheila tried to reason, "we're good, look." She pulled the media cards from her back pocket to show him. "We've got all we need right here." These were the electronic chips that held everything they'd shot so far.

The sight of the cards seemed to calm him. "Yes, fine," Giovanni muttered before he began coughing from the smoke.

"Let's start walking down," she suggested. "Come on."

"Of course. We don't need the truck. Let all that shit burn," he said with a wave of his hand.

That's when Sheila heard the low rumble.

At first she thought it was a helicopter, but as it grew louder she spotted the orange airplane, low over the treetops, coming straight at them.

"Incoming!" Deputy Martinez announced before she jumped into her squad car.

Sheila stood mesmerized by the approaching aircraft. Eddie, Tom, Luther, and Giovanni all watched it too.

Martinez opened her car door and shouted, "Take cover!" over the noise of the approaching prop plane.

Sheila then understood. "In here!" She turned and ducked into the back of the camera truck. Luther and Giovanni followed.

But Tom and Eddie hesitated, both standing outside, eyes on the crazy-looking orange aircraft seconds before it was upon them.

The water hit—drenching everything in an instant.

Tom and Eddie were knocked off their feet.

CHAPTER
TWENTY-THREE

Eddie got up and went to help Tom. He could see the actor was shaken and asked, "You all right, bro?"

"Son of a bitch!" Tom cursed.

Deputy Martinez emerged from the safety of her vehicle, stepped around a puddle, and squinted up at the smoldering trees.

"What the fuck?!" Tom shouted at her.

"The Superscooper," she explained, "dumping water sucked up from the San Gabriel Reservoir. Cal Fire is fighting the blaze north of here, but I didn't expect those boys here so fast," she said while studying the effectiveness of the drop.

"You could have warned us," Tom said.

"I gave instructions."

"You did not."

"Yes, I did," she said.

"Hardly."

"Sir, what part of 'Take cover' do you not understand?"

"You could have been more specific."

"We're lucky that wasn't fire retardant."

Tom continued in defiance. "*We're* lucky? *We?* You're not the one that's totally soaked here."

"If either of you are in need of medical attention—"

"I'm fine," Eddie said, trying to defuse the situation. "How about you?" he asked Tom. "You okay, bud? Anything hurt?"

"I don't know ... I don't think so. But I'm putting in for hazard pay," he said through clenched teeth.

Eddie laughed. Tom was referring to the bump in salary actors receive when they are asked to work in scenes involving elements such as water, snow, or theatrical smoke—not necessarily hazardous conditions, but that's how the Screen Actors Guild defines it.

"I'm fucking serious," Tom said to Eddie.

"Okay, but I'm soaked too. Where's my hazard pay?"

"Hell, you fucking directors sit back in video village sipping lattes most the time anyway. Where's the hazard in that?"

Eddie let it go. He could argue with Tom—but what's the point?

"Did it work?" Giovanni asked the deputy as he looked to the steam rising from the bank of trees.

Martinez said, "It just bought us some time before the fire crew gets here. Keep your eyes peeled. Those flyboys may scoop some more and come back."

Tom scanned the sky for the plane and said, "It better not come back," before he sat on the liftgate.

More time passed as they nervously waited in silence. Eddie could see the water drop had dampened the fire, and there was far less smoke coming from the trees, but it was starting to come back. Meanwhile Deputy Martinez was at her car talking on the radio. Giovanni and Luther stood off to the side speaking in hushed tones. Sheila was back in the truck, coughing, and she appeared to be dour and lost in thought. Eddie went to a nearby cooler and pulled out a handful of bottled waters. When he came back he caught her eye. "Want one?"

"Yeah, thanks," said Sheila.

He tossed it. She caught it with both hands and came out of the truck. He offered one to Tom who shook his head no. Eddie set the waters down on the liftgate and opened one for himself. The cold water felt good on his parched throat.

"This is so crazy," Sheila said.

"Yeah," Eddie said and asked Sheila, "You all right?"

She nodded, but he could tell she wasn't.

Tom said, "I've got to admit, the sight of blood totally freaks me out," before he took one of the bottles. He opened it, sipped, and added, "I could have never been a surgeon."

More time passed with few words between them.

Deputy Martinez returned from her car and said, "There are hot spots all over the range and this fire has stretched the sheriff's department's resources."

"What do you mean?" asked Tom.

"I won't have an officer to meet us at the Gold Strike for now. And, we'll likely have to evacuate from there."

"Oh, that's great," Tom said facetiously.

"Want a water?" Eddie asked the deputy.

"Thank you." She took one, opened it, and sipped.

"Where will we go if not the hotel?"

"Sheriff substation if we have to evacuate," she said, studying the smoke coming from the trees.

There was an awkward silence before Tom snapped, "Where's that van? It should be here by now."

Eddie said to Tom, "What do you say we dig up some dry clothes from the wardrobe trailer?"

"Good idea," Tom said.

"Make it quick," Martinez said. "I'll follow the van down when it returns and we'll reconvene at the hotel. From there I'll determine if we move again."

"Why can't we just go home?" Tom asked her.

"That's not how it's done."

"How what's done?"

"There's a been a murder. This is procedure."

Tom shook his head before he said, "Okay ... whatever you say."

Martinez dryly returned, "Your patience is very much appreciated, sir."

Eddie said to Tom, "Come on, Tom, let's get changed."

Eddie led the way. As they waddled to the wardrobe trailer, Eddie tried to calm Tom by changing the subject. "On one shoot, my crew and I were caught in a crazy rainstorm working in the Caribbean. Talk about wet. It rained so hard you couldn't hear yourself think. Destroyed equipment, all the electronic stuff mostly, the monitors. Now *that* was a living hell."

When they were out of earshot, Tom seethed, "That bitch could have warned us."

"You're right," Eddie said. "But who knew?"

"What she lacks in size she tries to make up for with a bitchy attitude. Classic Napoleon complex, I see it all the time."

In the wardrobe trailer Tom found the clothes he wore to set hanging on the door, khakis and a pullover sweatshirt. As he peeled off his costume, Eddie searched through boxes and came up with Dockers and a flannel shirt that looked like they'd fit. Unseen by Tom, he snuck the mini bottles of vodka out of his wet jeans and slid them into the front pocket of the khakis. *Just in case.*

"Ever been on set when someone died before?" Tom asked Eddie as they got dressed.

"No."

"I was on a horror film in Wisconsin, years ago, when I first was starting out and living in New York. *Zipperface II.* The effects guy blew himself up."

"How?"

"He was setting a charge of gasoline for a car explosion. Back then, lots of movies had cars exploding. Remember that? Always made it in the film's trailer. It must have been a spark or something.

The worst part … you could smell the guy. I don't know if you've ever experienced that, but burning flesh smells really horrible. Like … evil. The fire extinguisher didn't work so they had to put him out with sound blankets. His hands were all charred and curled up," Tom demonstrated, making claws with his fingers.

"Oh, man."

"It's weird, but sometimes I catch a whiff of something and it brings me back to that night. Olfactory memory is what they call it. I get that whiff and can remember it all, everything … what the guy was wearing, his screams."

"Horrible."

"We were only a week in so everyone just went home and they never finished the movie. A shame, too, because I had a good role."

Eddie wondered if that would be the fate of this film, if Sam would throw in the towel since they were already so far behind schedule.

Story of my life, he thought.

Tom finished dressing and said, "But this is different. That wrangler guy was murdered, like the deputy said. That was no accident. He was killed and stuffed in the stagecoach."

"You're saying the killer was trying to hide him?"

"Exactly. And my question is," Tom said, "who started that fire?" He looked out the window of the trailer.

"Someone doesn't want us here," Eddie said.

Tom looked out the window nervously before he said, "Where the fuck is that van?"

"You see those financiers?" Eddie said.

"The suits wearing Italian loafers? Yeah."

"Don't say anything, but Sam admitted to me he suspects they're Mob."

"Russian Mob?"

"I guess. He met them in New York. This movie is being financed all through cash, and …" Eddie said, fearing he'd said too much.

"Okay," Tom said, waiting for Eddie to elaborate.

"Maybe someone's trying to get back at them."

"By spoiling their investment," Tom said.

"Or by sending a message. Like *The Godfather*, with the horse head in the bed."

"Do you think Patches breaking her leg was no accident?"

"I don't know. Maybe it's just my active imagination, but ..." Then Eddie remembered the old geezer, Chuck, selling beef jerky on the side of the road. He asked Tom, "Did you see that old dude at the jerky stand on the way up here?"

"What dude?"

Eddie explained how he, Giovanni, Sheila, John, and Paul had all pulled over to a roadside stand and that he'd thought the guy had an interesting look, with mutton chop sideburns, and had invited him to be an extra. "The old guy seemed a bit eccentric, but not crazy. You never know."

Tom asked, "You think the jerky he's selling is not beef? Something else?"

"Cannibalism?"

"Sort of a *Texas Chainsaw Massacre* thing."

"Hadn't thought of that," Eddie said, trying to remember if he had sampled the jerky.

"You tell the deputy about him?"

"Just thought of it now."

"I bet she knows the guy," Tom said, eyeing Martinez out the window. "She probably fraternizes with all the hillbillies living up here."

"I'll ask," Eddie said. "But wouldn't a cannibal come back for his trophy?"

"What do you mean?"

"If he's killing to stock his supply, he'd need the body, right? He wouldn't stuff it in the stagecoach. He'd haul it back and gut it, then salt and dry the meat out in the sun, or something ..."

"Unless he's saving it for later."

"Maybe."

"But why the horse wrangler?"

"The guy was probably just out tending to ..." Eddie started in and then stopped himself, remembering, "Wait a minute ... his assistant, Lucky."

"Who?"

"That other wrangler. The weird one. He was showing me these snakes he'd brought, trying to get them in the movie and Jimmy came up and reprimanded him."

"I saw snakes in an old pickup when I checked into the hotel," Tom remembered.

"Those are rattlesnakes." Eddie explained his encounter and the conflict between Jimmy and Lucky.

"So ... where are these snakes now?" Tom asked.

"I don't know."

That's when they heard Sheila's scream.

Then gunshots.

They shared a look: *What was that?*

Eddie burst out of the trailer only to see Deputy Martinez with an arrow lodged in her thigh. She had her gun drawn and was firing out into the woods. She emptied the pistol's clip and was reaching into her belt when another arrow struck her below the Adam's apple. The impact spun the deputy around. Eddie could see the arrow was now sticking out of her back, protruding from her lower neck—skewered like a shish kebab.

Tom came up beside Eddie and said, "Holy shit!"

Giovanni, Sheila, and Luther cowered while Martinez, in full battle mode, continued to fire into the trees. The deputy stumbled to her patrol car when a third arrow struck her in the tailbone. She let out a yelp and fell forward, dropping into the muddy gravel.

"Holy shit!" Tom yelled.

The deputy was flopping like a fish out of water as Eddie moved in to help her. The next arrow whizzed past his head. It popped into the trailer behind him.

I'm next, Eddie thought.

"Fuck this!" Tom exclaimed before he ran for the cover of Tami's trailer.

CHAPTER
TWENTY-FOUR

Martinez had emptied her second clip and was trying to get to the radio when she realized she couldn't speak. The arrow lodged in her throat had crushed her windpipe and blood filled her mouth. When she tried to call out only a gurgle was possible.

Get the shotgun.

Next came the sharp pain in her lower back. Her legs gave way. There was the sensation of her face hitting the gravel as blood and bile came up from her stomach. She gasped for air.

Locate the threat. She'd been trained for this.

Martinez lifted her head, searched the trees but could see nothing. As much as she tried, it was impossible to get back to her feet, her legs useless. She feared the last arrow might have severed her spine. She'd seen those types of injuries, car accident victims. Or hopefully she was just in shock.

The horizon swirled.

If this was it, if this was how she'd die … she aimed the Glock where she thought the killer might be.

Breathe.

The pain was overwhelming, but Martinez had been there before, during childbirth. Nothing could compare.

Stay strong.

Multiple images flashed through her mind.

One moment she was in the hospital giving birth to Cesar. For some reason, in her mind's eye, the pattern on the ceiling of the delivery room was above her now. Next, she was at peace and holding baby Cesar, the infant wrapped in a blanket, his eyes staring back at her in wonder. Next Cesar was the fussing toddler. Martinez was dressing him for church and putting on a clip-on tie.

The image of the Velvet Elvis came to her mind. But now Elvis' tears were real, not just painted, actual streams running down the black velvet.

Now Cesar was standing in Mrs. Gomez's apartment—*I'll be home soon, baby.* Martinez reached out.

Then all went black.

CHAPTER
TWENTY-FIVE

Tom dove into Tami's trailer and ducked at the base of the kitchen cabinets. *Shit!* He lay flat on the carpet and could hear the others shouting in panic outside. A moment later they all came bursting inside.

A loud crack sounded just above Tom's head. Another arrow had shattered one of the trailer windows, shards of glass raining down on his head.

"It's coming from the trees," Giovanni screamed.

With everyone inside the trailer, Tom jumped up, pulled the door shut, and locked it tight. All spread out, hunched low, eyes glued out the windows. Tom could see the wounded deputy lying in the gravel, gun clenched in her hand, arrows sticking out of her as if she were a pincushion. He couldn't believe his eyes and blurted out, "They killed a cop!"

"Did you see who it was?" asked Eddie.

"No," Tom replied.

"You guys?" Eddie asked the others.

"No," Giovanni said.

Sheila shook her head, speechless.

Luther barked, "Shit!" Then, shouting out the broken window, he screamed, "Motherfucker!" He went from window to window, face red with anger, adrenaline peaking.

Tom asked, "What happened?"

Voice cracking, Sheila attempted to explain what she'd just witnessed. "One second the deputy was talking to us and everything was fine. The next she was hit by an arrow and started shooting. Then there were more arrows, and ..."

"Who was she shooting at?" Tom asked.

"I couldn't see."

"Did anyone see anything?" asked Eddie.

There was a moment of silence before a loud pop made Tom flinch. Another arrow—this one puncturing the trailer as if it were mere cardboard. He stared at the black projectile lodged into the wooden kitchen cabinet above his head, the feathered end vibrating like a pitchfork.

"Motherfucker!" Luther screamed.

Tom wished he had run into the woods instead of hiding in the trailer. "This is a death trap, he said. "We're surrounded."

"Why are they trying to kill us?" sounded Giovanni.

Tom stated the obvious. "Someone doesn't want us here."

"Who?" asked Sheila.

Nobody had an answer. Everyone peered out the windows for a clue.

"I'm going for the deputy's gun," Luther said, pointing to her fallen body near the squad car.

"Don't do anything stupid," Giovanni said, but it was too late. Luther threw the bolt on the door and was out.

"Luther!"

From the window, Tom could see Luther run toward the fallen deputy, then drop and scurry commando-style. "That kid's crazy," he said.

Luther was about halfway there when an arrow struck him in the hip. He cursed and reached back to grab hold of the shaft.

"Get back here!" Giovanni yelled.

Resilient, Luther tried to pull the arrow out, face scrunching in pain, but finally gave up. He pressed forward until he reached Deputy Martinez. Luther pried the pistol from her hand and turned back. Another arrow flew past, missing him as he hobbled, the arrow lodged in his hip slowing his progress. Halfway back to the trailer, another arrow struck him in the back. He arched and cried out.

"Luther!" Giovanni screamed.

But Luther kept moving, determined. He stumbled inside the trailer and Tom slammed the door behind him, locking it.

Luther held up the pistol victoriously, and, gasping for air, said, "I got it," before he fell to his knees.

Giovanni cried, "Why'd you do that?"

Luther gave Giovanni the pistol, tears in his eyes, and replied, "I got it for you."

"I didn't ask you to—"

Then Luther coughed blood, the crimson expulsion staining the white carpet.

Giovanni gasped.

Tom could see how uncomfortable Giovanni was holding the Glock, so he took it from him. The pistol was still warm from having been fired moments ago.

"Probably a punctured lung," Eddie said, helping Giovanni prop Luther up to a sitting position.

"How can you tell?" Sheila asked.

"Blood in his windpipe," Eddie said.

Tears in his eyes, Luther coughed more blood and leaned over. He moaned as a stream poured from the side of his mouth, the deep red in stark contrast against the white carpet.

"Nobody asked you to be the hero," an emotional Giovanni said. "Why did you do that?"

Luther heaved, trying to catch his breath.

In frustration, Tom snapped, "Where's that fucking passenger van?" He hated that he had been forced to give up his seat on the first run.

"Know how to use that thing?" Eddie asked, motioning to the gun in Tom's hand.

"Sure," Tom lied. In truth, he'd only shot a gun in a play once, a prop gun loaded with blanks. *How different could it be?*

"Keep an eye out," Eddie said, motioning to the window.

Tom turned his attention out to the woods. He thought he saw something moving and aimed out the window but smoke from the fire hindered his visibility. *Where are they?*

"These arrows," Sheila said, kneeled at Luther's side, "it's freaky that they're so powerful … that they go right through this trailer."

"We're not safe in here," Tom said.

Eddie asked, "What was it that the Park Ranger said? Something about Vaseline on the tip?"

"Makes them penetrate deeper," Tom remembered. "What kind of crazy fuck—" he started to say when another arrow slammed through the trailer. Tom flinched then instinctively fired out the window. He didn't see anything but wanted to let the killer know they had a gun.

"What'd you see?" Sheila asked.

The smell of burnt powder flared Tom's nostrils before he admitted, "Nothing," surprised by the kick of the 9 millimeter. It was considerably more substantial than the recoil he'd remembered from firing the prop gun in that stage play.

"Save the rounds," Eddie said. "We may need them."

"Who made you the boss?"

"I'm just saying that—"

"I know what I'm doing."

Eddie said nothing in return. Instead, he helped Giovanni with a towel in an attempt to slow Luther's bleeding.

Tom returned his attention to the window, studied the woods before he said, "It's so weird nobody saw anything."

Giovanni consoled Luther gently, "Try to relax. We're going to get you help."

Luther moaned in pain, gasping for air.

Tom had to look away. He turned to Eddie and asked, "Think it's that old man?"

"What old man?" Sheila questioned.

"The roadside jerky guy," Tom said, and then back to Eddie, "Tell 'em your theory."

"I was saying to Tom, maybe it's that jerky guy mad at us for some reason."

"Why would *he* be mad?" Sheila said.

"I don't know."

"Or maybe it's cannibalism," Tom offered.

"Cannibalism?" Sheila questioned.

"Possibly," Eddie said. "Maybe that beef jerky is actually—"

"Someone's coming!" Tom snapped. Out the window he eyed a beat-up pickup truck with a camper shell driving into base camp. Tom trained the gun on the truck and said, "Who's that?"

"The jerky guy," Sheila said.

"He's the killer?" Tom asked.

"Don't know, but that's his truck," Eddie said.

All were silent and watched as the pickup came to a stop. The driver side door opened and, as if on cue, jerky proprietor Chuck emerged. He scratched his white sideburns and looked around.

"It's him," Sheila whispered.

The old man stood with a confused look on his face. From his position, fallen Martinez was out of sight, lying on the other side of the squad car. He scanned the surroundings and said aloud, "Hello!" Chuck then squinted in their direction. It appeared as if he'd noticed them hidden in the trailer.

"Shit, he sees us," Tom said. He aimed the Glock as the old man approached. *I'll kill him*, Tom figured. Because the guy was moving, he was not certain he could get a clean shot, so he waited. *What's that saying from American history in school? The whites of their eyes?* Then the old man stopped and looked beyond them as if sensing something was not quite right.

"What's he doing?" Sheila said.

Now that the jerky guy had stopped moving, Tom was pretty sure he could hit him. He had the sights lined on the man's chest. He was about to squeeze the trigger when an arrow struck Chuck in the upper chest. The old man cried out, grasped the shaft with one hand. His knees quivered and he dropped.

Tom lowered the Glock with, "Holy shit!"

CHAPTER
TWENTY-SIX

Sheila couldn't watch. She had to turn away as the old man cried out in anguish. She couldn't stand to see another person die. It was so cruel and senseless. Chuck's cries seemed to agitate Luther, who wheezed in labored breath before he coughed up even more discharge. Sheila assumed Luther must be drowning in his own blood, felt helpless that they couldn't do anything to help him.

"We need to go get that guy," Eddie proposed.

"You can, but I'm staying here," Tom said.

A minute later Chuck fell silent.

"We go for that pickup," Sheila suggested.

Kneeling by Luther, Giovanni said, "I don't know if we can move him."

Sheila considered Luther for a moment before she said, "Take the gun and give us cover. We'll get the truck and pull up alongside the trailer." She could see from the look on Tom's face that he didn't like the idea. It appeared the actor had grown possessive of the 9 millimeter Glock.

"What makes you think we can make it to the truck?" Tom questioned.

"They can't hit us all," she said. "We make a scattered break for it."

"They?"

"Or he … it may be more than one," she said, searching for a clue out the window.

"And take our chances? That's crazy," Tom said.

Eddie said, "I say some of us can go for the truck and others go for the patrol car. At the same time."

"What if the keys aren't in either?" Tom said.

Sheila considered that before she said, "They've got to be in either the ignition or the pocket of the driver."

"Yeah … well, that archer is one hell of a shot," Tom reminded all. "We saw what happened to Luther. Taking the time to dig keys out of that old man's pocket … you're a sitting duck. It's a death sentence for sure."

"Maybe he's still alive," Eddie said. "He can tell us where they are."

Sheila peered outside to see the old man curled up in a fetal position, motionless. "It's the chance we've got to take," she said.

"You guys can go but I'm staying right here," Tom said, holding up the Glock. "Sooner or later someone will come for us."

"What about Luther?" Giovanni said. "He needs help. We've got to get him to a hospital."

Tom replied, "You guys can do whatever you want, but death by grease-tipped arrow is not in my job description."

"We've all got to stick together," Sheila said. There was a moment of tense silence as she, Tom, Eddie, and Giovanni considered each other. Luther had begun to slip in and out of consciousness.

"Who is it that's trying to kill us?" Giovanni said with frustration. "And why? It's crazy."

"Maybe Sheila's right and it's more than one," Eddie said.

More silence as they scanned the surroundings outside the trailer. Sheila said, "It's like they're invisible."

"Camouflage," Eddie said. "That's what bowhunters do. They wear camo and cover their scent because they're so up close to their prey."

"This kind of crazy shit would never happen in Italy," Giovanni said. "It's like ... *Fort Apache* or something."

"Never saw that movie," Eddie confided.

"I saw *Fort Apache, the Bronx*," said Tom.

"Not the same thing," Giovanni replied.

"Okay, look," Sheila said, "when the van comes back we make a break for it. We all run at once."

"What if the van never comes back?" Eddie uttered.

"Firefighters. They're bound to show up, right?" Tom said. "The deputy called it in, and that airplane dropped water."

"It makes sense they'd come," Eddie said, "but who knows. They could be stretched thin with that fire everywhere, protecting homes and businesses. You've seen the local news covering forest fires. That's what they do first."

Luther offered a whimper before he squeaked out, "I don't want to die."

Giovanni said, "We've got to get him to the hospital now. I'll go for the truck." He knelt down close to Luther and softly said, "We're going to get you out of here. Hang in there, okay?"

"I'll go too," Sheila offered.

"Me too," Eddie said and added, "We split up and go for both the sheriff's car and the pickup at the same time." He gave Sheila a nod. She felt it was a good plan but hoped they wouldn't be lambs heading to the slaughter.

"Okay," she said, but then heard a low rumble. "Wait ... listen ..."

"The Superscooper," Tom said with a tinge of hatred. "It's back."

Although Sheila couldn't see the aircraft, the familiar propeller noise grew louder and louder. All trained their ears until it was upon them. The sudden downpour rocked the trailer. The corrugated tin roof only amplified the sound of the thundering deluge. As the sound of the aircraft faded away Sheila peered out the window, water streaming down from the roof, to see a blanket of steamy white mist hanging in the air.

"They know we're here so firefighters will come," Tom said.

Sheila could see a plume of smoke billowing from the doused trees. It appeared as if the wind had changed direction and a white smoke drifted toward them now. It was an eerie cloud, like a demonic fog. It engulfed both the deputy and the jerky guy. Seconds later Sheila could not see more than twenty feet beyond the trailer. "That water created a smokescreen," she said. "If we go now, the killer can't see us."

Eddie gazed out the window and said, "That's right. They can't shoot what they can't see."

"You guys are nuts," Tom said.

"Watch the trees," Sheila said to Tom, "If you see something take a shot, but whatever you do don't shoot us."

Peering out the window, Tom said, "I can't see for shit."

Sheila unlocked the door. Motioning to the pistol in Tom's hand she asked, "Are you sure you can you handle that?"

"I guess so."

"Guess?"

"I've got your back," Tom said, unconvincing.

"Maybe one of us should take it," Sheila suggested.

"You're going to need your hands," Tom said, protective of the gun, not willing to give it up.

"Just don't shoot us," she insisted.

"I won't."

"Whoever gets their vehicle started first," Eddie said, "pull it up over here by the door." He pointed to the area just outside the steps of the trailer. "We'll load Luther and get the hell out of there. But don't leave without all of us together. There's strength in numbers. We drive down together. Agreed?"

"Sounds like a good plan," Giovanni said.

Eddie dug into his pocket. He came up with two mini vodka bottles.

Where'd he get those? Sheila thought. *Was he on a flight?*

Eddie held the bottles up and said, "For luck, and a wee bit of courage." He twisted off the cap and offered one to her. Sheila shook her head no, so he offered it to Giovanni who waved it off.

"You sure?" Eddie asked.

"No, thank you, my friend," Giovanni said.

"I'll take one," Tom said.

"But you're not going out there."

Tom waved his fingers with a "gimme" gesture.

Eddie handed him the mini vodka bottle, "It's what kamikaze pilots do. *Kanpai*," he said before downing his.

Tom took a cautious sip, said, "But this is *not* saki."

"Next best thing," Eddie managed to say as he tapped at his chest, the vodka seemingly burning its way down his windpipe.

"You guys are crazy," Sheila said.

"Sure as hell," Eddie said with a wry smile. He carefully set the empty bottle on the counter.

Tom finished his and tossed the mini bottle before checking the gun.

Meanwhile, Giovanni tenderly stroked Luther's blond hair. "I'll be back for you," he whispered, and kissed him on the forehead. Then Giovanni was back on his feet.

"Ready?" Sheila asked.

Eddie and Giovanni nodded.

"You go for the sheriff's car," Sheila said to Eddie, "and we'll go for the pickup."

"Got it."

"You good?" Giovanni asked Eddie.

He nodded, yes.

Sheila inhaled deeply, her palms sweaty. She could feel her heart pumping in her chest as she turned to Tom to remind him, "Please, don't shoot us."

"I won't."

She turned back. "Let's do it."

Eddie led the way as they burst out the door.

CHAPTER
TWENTY-SEVEN

Eddie couldn't see the patrol car; the smoke was too thick. Instead, he relied on his sense of direction, where he thought it might be. His eyes burned from the acrid smoke and he could hear the others coughing off to his left.

First, he came across the deputy, multiple arrows piercing her body. Then he could see the vehicle. Hunched low, Eddie dashed for the driver's-side door. The keys were not in the ignition. *Shit.*

He scrambled back to the deputy, pushed aside the shaft of an arrow sticking out of her lower back and reached into her khakis. Her body was still warm and he was close enough to smell her sweat. He half-expected her to awaken and sit up, but she didn't move. Realizing this was a dead body, he coughed up a mouthful of bile in disgust but swallowed it back. It tasted like the vodka he'd downed only moments ago.

Eddie found a set of keys in her pocket and pulled them out. On the keychain there was a photo of a young boy.

That's when he felt the breeze.

The wind had changed direction.

It became painfully obvious when the smoke cleared that suddenly his security blanket, the smokescreen, was gone. By then Eddie could see Giovanni and Sheila climb into the pickup truck.

There was a barking dog. Sheila and Giovanni jumped out. Rosie the pit bull sprung out of the cab and gave chase.

The animal nipped at Giovanni's heels and he tumbled forward. The dog attacked, teeth snapping ferocious. Giovanni kicked at her. The pit bull was determined not to give up. It had Giovanni's calf in its jaws and was yanking its head violently from side to side. He screamed.

Pulling on the dog's hind leg, Sheila tried to pull the animal away but had little effect. The dog then turned on her. This gave Giovanni the chance to struggle to his feet. The dog spun and snarled between them.

A shot rang out.

Eddie could see Tom's arm sticking out the window of the trailer, gun trained. A second shot followed and the dog yelped, tumbled backward. The third and fourth shot missed, kicking up dirt, and the dog retreated.

Don't waste bullets, Eddie thought.

The vengeful pit bull found shelter under her master's pickup.

Giovanni was cursing when an arrow struck him in the middle of the chest. The impact sent him back on his heels and there was a surprised expression on his face.

Sheila screamed. She went for him just as a second arrow struck Giovanni under the chin. That one snapped his head back. His arms flailed skyward and he dropped. Sheila screamed again and ran for the trailer.

Eddie tried to follow the trajectory. The arrows, where did they come from? He scanned the trees but could see nothing.

Get the car.

He jumped in and fumbled with the keys. A loud pop sounded. He knew an arrow had penetrated the siding of the vehicle but couldn't see where. The cruiser started with a roar and he threw it into gear. Eddie maneuvered the squad car around to the trailer. He pulled up alongside and threw it into park.

There was a shotgun in a center rack but it was locked.

Eddie pulled the keys from the ignition and searched for one that might fit the lock. He found a small brass key that looked promising, popped open the lock, and retrieved the Remington pump-action shotgun.

He jumped out of the car and aimed the shotgun into the trees but could still see nothing. When he went for the trailer, he was surprised to discover the door locked. "Let me in!" he shouted.

An arrow slammed into the trailer's corrugated siding beside him just before Sheila unlocked and opened the door. Eddie burst inside.

"Holy shit!" Tom said as Eddie stumbled in.

Sheila slammed the door and locked it. "Giovanni's been hit!" she said, eyes full of tears.

"Where'd that fucking dog come from?!" asked Tom.

"It's the jerky guy's," Eddie said. "We saw it before, at his roadside stand."

"I capped that fucking mongrel," Tom said with pride.

Eddie instructed, "Let's get Luther in the car. I'll give you guys cover," he said, holding up the shotgun. "Load Luther and we'll pull around for Giovanni."

Tom pointed to Luther lying on the carpet, "I think he's dead."

Eddie set the shotgun down and kneeled to check on Luther.

Tom continued, "I say we leave him and get the hell out of here."

Eddie could see no signs of life. Maybe Luther was gone. He couldn't tell.

Sheila said, "We can't just leave him here."

"Of course we can," Tom said.

"What about Giovanni?"

"Same deal. We get the hell out of here and call for help."

"We're not leaving without Giovanni," she snapped. She went

to the window to see how he was doing.

"He's probably dead too," Tom said. "Or will be soon."

"You don't know that," she said.

"What I do know is that killer is one hell of a shot. I'm not going to be the next."

Looking out the window at his fallen friend, Eddie said, "We're bringing both of them. We'll get down to the Gold Strike and—"

"Fuck that!" Tom said, "I'm not risking my life just to get a pair of two-hundred-pound dead guys down the hill."

"They're not dead," Sheila barked back.

"They're both dead."

"I'm not leaving him."

"Missy," Tom said, losing his patience, "Face it. Our cameraman is dead. He's like a beetle stuck to cardboard and we can't help him." He pointed to Luther, "And surfer boy here stopped breathing. We'll let the cops come back for them, but we need to get out of here."

Sheila was not convinced. As they continued to argue, Eddie went back to Luther, the carpet surrounding him soaked in blood. Maybe Tom was right. Luther didn't appear to be breathing. There might be nothing they could do. He checked for a pulse, felt nothing, then went to the window to consider Giovanni. The smoke had drifted away but something else caught Eddie's eye—the corpse of Deputy Martinez. It seemed different than before. She was now face down, not like he'd left her. Arrows were no longer protruding from her body. "Wait a minute," he said, "the arrows are gone."

"What arrows?" said Tom.

"The sheriff … I was just there, getting the keys, and …"

"And what?"

"The arrows have been pulled out and her body has been moved."

"You sure about that?" Tom peered out the window.

"Yes."

"The killer has only so many arrows," Sheila reasoned.

Eddie nodded. "He's retrieving them."

"Then why didn't we see—?" Tom started in before he was cut off by the sound of a loud pop outside the trailer, a much different sound than that of the arrows penetrating the trailer's siding. It startled everyone and was followed by the sound of a hiss. "What's that?"

"The deputy's car," Eddie said, "the tires."

CHAPTER TWENTY-EIGHT

Tom was enraged they'd wasted so much time. He said, "We can still get out of here with flat tires. We'll ride the rims like they do on TV car chases."

Another pop sounded. Tom went to the window, aimed the Glock but saw nothing. With raised shotgun, Eddie took position at the window next to him. "See anything?"

"No," Tom said.

"Okay," Sheila said, "we leave the guys behind for now and make a break for it. But we're coming back."

"We will," Eddie promised.

"You guys can come back, not me," said Tom.

"We go for the car all at the same time. Stay low," Eddie said.

Tom reached for the cowboy hat—the same hat he was not allowed to wear in the movie. Tom checked himself out in the mirror and adjusted the brim. He was glad he'd left it behind in Tami's trailer.

"You ready, Tex?" Eddie asked.

"Don't patronize me," Tom said.

Eddie gave Tom the thumbs-up.

Tom hated him.

"What's that smell?" Sheila said.

Tom could see black smoke coming from the bathroom and caught the scent of burning rubber. When it became apparent what was happening, he said, "They're burning us out."

Eddie went to a window and peered out. "Why can't I see anybody?"

"It's time, let's do it," Sheila said and turned to Eddie, "Can you cover us?" nodding to the shotgun.

"Sam Peckinpah style," Eddie said.

"Who?"

"Not important. I got your back."

"Don't do anything stupid," she said.

"Define stupid."

Tom coughed and said, "Let's get the fuck out of here before we die from smoke inhalation."

Eddie kicked open the door and fired the shotgun. It was loud and Tom could feel the percussion in his chest. Sheila followed him out. Tom clenched his teeth and was the last out the door.

Tom hunched low and trained his pistol under the trailer looking for the killer but nobody was there. He waved the Glock at nothing in particular before he went for the patrol car.

Eddie jumped in the driver's side.

Sheila hopped in the passenger seat.

Tom went for the back seat. He yanked the door handle but it was locked. *Shit!* Totally exposed, he could hear that crazy dog barking again. Sheila, inside the vehicle, turned back and was trying to unlock the back door but the prisoner partition between the front and back seats made it impossible.

Tom gave up and went for the front door. He jumped in. It was a tight fit but he managed to close the door seconds before the ferocious animal was there and snarling beside them.

The car whirred, gained traction, and was in motion. Eddie maneuvered it around the trailer and veered it up the embankment. The vehicle lurched and bounced. Tom's head smacked against the side window.

They were making progress, but suddenly there was a crunching sound, clearly rocks scraping the floorboards. The car trembled and came to a stop. Tom could hear the back wheels whir.

"The flat tires, we have no clearance," Eddie said. He yanked the shifter into reverse and gunned it. This strategy only rocked the car back and forth but did nothing to free the vehicle.

Tom could see they were stuck. *Fuck!*

An arrow slammed into the passenger-side door window. Safety glass shattered and instantly covered Tom's lap. He wasn't going to die like this, a sitting duck.

Tom climbed out of the car and ran for the trees.

The dog came at him.

Tom gritted his teeth, aimed the pistol, and fired. The impact from the 9 millimeter snapped the dog's head back before it fell in a heap, silenced forever.

He fired again, for good measure, but was then out of bullets. *Fuck me!*

Tom ran.

Before he reached the trees, Tom could hear the car doors slam behind him. He turned back to see Eddie and Sheila running the other direction. *That's right, split up.*

He ran into the woods.

Tom zig-zagged his way through the thick foliage, then came across a cable ladder hanging under a pine. Following it up, Tom saw the platform rigged on a branch above. It appeared to be some sort of makeshift support contraption and Tom wondered what it could be. The deck was made out of speed rail and pieces of scaffolding he'd seen the grips use for camera support. There was a foldable chair from the lunch tent, ropes, and mountain-climbing equipment tied off, even a plastic bottle of drinking water.

Upon closer inspection, he could see a sheath full of arrows.

It dawned on him—this is a makeshift hunter's perch. The entire time he'd been searching for the killer at ground level, but no, the arrows had come from the trees above. That's why he never saw anyone.

Where's the killer now?

Tom ran for his life.

CHAPTER
TWENTY-NINE

Sheila ran ahead as she and Eddie made their way down the dirt road. She wouldn't allow him to slow her progress. *He can fend for himself.*

She ran a good ten minutes before she rounded the bend and was surprised to see Don's passenger van flipped over on its side, nestled into a roadside ditch. She slowed to a walking pace which gave Eddie time to reach her. They studied the wreckage, catching their breaths. Eddie said, "No wonder why the van never came back." He aimed the shotgun at the van and brushed past her.

"What do you think happened?" she said.

"Looks like it was heading back up and …" she could see Eddie stammer at the sight of something. Sheila approached. He held up his hand to halt her progress. "You don't want to see this."

"What?"

"Trust me."

Sheila ignored him and came up anyway. Don the driver was splayed over the dash. His throat had been slashed from ear to ear. A large kitchen knife was lodged under his jawbone, its black handle protruding out. Splattered blood drenched the windshield.

Eddie lowered the shotgun and said, "Throat slashed while he was driving."

"So, the killer was behind him," Sheila said.

"One of the passengers."

Sheila swallowed hard, said, "I don't get it."

"It was one of us," he said.

"What was?"

"Don was driving back to get us. He was attacked from behind, someone in the passenger seat."

"What makes you think it was someone from the crew?"

"I doubt he would have picked up a stranger."

"But ... maybe the killer was hiding behind the seats."

"And snuck on after everyone was dropped off at the Gold Strike? I doubt it."

Sheila tried to envision it. Even though she was sweating, she felt an icy chill. She wondered aloud, "Who from the crew would want to kill us all?" She tried to recall if anyone fit the profile, adding, "It doesn't make sense."

"We should keep moving," he said, glancing back over his shoulder.

He was right. She felt they'd spent too much time standing there even though it had only been a minute. She scanned the woods, said, "We'll stay off the road and make our way down in the trees. If help comes we can run out and flag them down."

Eddie agreed before taking one last look at Don hunched over in a pool of blood. "Poor bastard," he said. "He was coming back for us."

They moved on. Sheila led the way as they hugged the tree line adjacent to the dirt road. Since the thick foliage slowed their progress, Eddie was able to keep up. She asked, "Where do you think Tom went?"

"I saw him running up the hill."

Sheila thought about what she'd just seen and felt sick to her stomach that Giovanni, her best friend, was now dead. The grim reality was so horrible she tried to not think about it. She said, "Assuming your theory is right, that the killer is someone employed on the film ... what would their motive be?"

"Revenge," Eddie replied.

"Revenge for what?"

"Who knows? Did you get the feeling anyone on the crew was pissed off?" he asked.

"Other than me?"

"What are you mad about?"

"Everything," she said. "I should have never taken this job but Giovanni asked me to," saddened that her friend was gone. "My mom just passed away and ..."

"Your mom in that assisted-living place?"

"That's right."

"The place you hate so much."

"Yeah. How do you know about it?"

"You told me," he said, "the night of the wrap party."

"Oh, right ..." Sheila couldn't remember mentioning her mother to him.

Eddie said, "You told me how great your mom was, raising you alone like she did, without any help. You said you guys were a great team and that only now, as an adult, did you realize she'd put her own dreams aside so you could pursue yours."

"I said that?"

"You don't remember?"

"Sort of. I guess ... I was really drunk that night."

"I could tell you loved her."

"She's the only family I've ever had," Sheila said with a hint of sadness, a bitter reminder that now she was all alone.

"She must have been proud of you."

"I guess."

Eddie said, "My mom thinks I'm a bum, wonders why I don't have a real job."

"But you're a director."

"She'd rather I sell out for a weekly paycheck, a stuffy corporate job with two weeks' vacation and a 401(k) like my brother. Maybe she's right. I am a bum."

"You're not a bum."

"Definitely a ne'er-do-well, and the prodigal son in my family."

"Don't be so hard on yourself," Sheila said. "You've got a career."

"Hardly. I can't catch a break to save my life."

"Tell me about it."

Eddie said, "It's great that you were so close to your mother. You'll always have that. A foundation."

Sheila said nothing more as they made their way down the hill. She wanted to go home but she didn't have one. She'd move out because it was Lisa's apartment, and under Santa Monica rent control so it was reasonably priced. Sheila would have to get her own apartment and start anew but she knew she couldn't afford Santa Monica. There was a little money in her mom's bank account. Once that became available maybe she'd have enough for the first month's rent and a security deposit, hopefully on the West Side, possibly in Mar Vista or Culver City.

When they reached a clearing, she saw a pickup truck ahead. She halted Eddie, pointed it out.

He eyed it for a moment and said, "That's Lucky's truck," Eddie raised the shotgun and they cautiously approached. She could see the sixties-era vintage truck was pulled over on the side of the road but there was nobody in the cab. Eddie moved out onto the open dirt road to investigate. Meanwhile Sheila scanned the woods, wondering if this truck could be bait for an ambush—the killer lying in wait.

Eddie turned back and said, "Nobody."

When Sheila felt it was safe, she emerged from the trees and ventured, "Maybe the keys are in it." Eddie peeked into the truck bed, and she went for the driver's-side door. When she opened it, rattlesnakes sounded and Lucky fell out.

Sheila screamed and jumped back.

The lifeless assistant wrangler was covered in his own vomit. One of the vipers was tangled in Lucky's dirty blue jeans. A few dropped from the truck's floorboard and onto the dirt road while a cacophony of rattles clattered within the truck cab. Sheila could see broken shards of glass from what looked like a fish aquarium on the upholstered bench seat.

Eddie gave the snakes on the ground a wide berth before he managed to slam the door of the pickup. A pair of diamondbacks slithered underneath the pickup but one was still tangled around Lucky's body.

"His own snakes," Eddie said.

Sheila considered Lucky's bloated face and the puncture wounds on his cheeks. "Where'd they come from?"

"He brought them. They were his pride and joy, the crazy bastard."

"Why rattlesnakes?"

"Who knows? They're rescue snakes," he said.

"What?"

He gave her a nod.

"Like … rescue dogs?"

"Exactly. He wanted me to put them in the movie."

"Do you think he's dead?"

Eddie prodded Lucky with the barrel of the shotgun. "Don't know, but it sure as hell looks like it."

She considered one of the snakes coiled under the truck and asked, "Do you think we can open the doors, clear them out, and take the truck?"

"I'm not going in that cab," he said. "Who knows how many are in there."

Sheila had images of snakes hidden under the old seat. "Yeah … makes sense," she said.

"Maybe someone broke that aquarium on purpose," Eddie said.

"Not an accident?"

"Nothing today has been an accident."

She felt a cool shiver up her spine. She felt naked standing out in the open road and said, "We should keep moving."

"Yeah."

"Snakes totally freak me out," she confessed as they found cover back in the trees. "Who would keep those things as pets?"

"I had a lizard when I was a kid, a chameleon," he said. "I fed it lettuce and special mealworms that came in plastic containers full of sawdust we bought at the pet store."

"But that's a lizard, not a deadly rattlesnake."

"I guess so. The lizard turned either brown or green. I had construction paper in each color leaned against the cage to demonstrate the magic. Then one day it stopped moving and turned black. My older sister said it was dead, but I wouldn't accept it, thought it was sleeping. My mom knew the lizard was a goner but she humored me and let me keep it for a couple days more. Finally, when it hadn't moved in a week or eaten any of the mealworms I'd offered and began to smell, I realized my sister was right. We put it in a jewelry box and buried it in my backyard. Held a mini funeral and everything."

With the talk of living things changing color, Sheila thought about her mother's skin tone as she died. Thoughts of her mother brought to mind the pet she'd had as a child. "We had an old cat," she said, "died when I was away at school. It was really sad. My mom called to tell me and I didn't want to cry in front of my dorm roommates, so I took a shower and let myself have a cry under the spray. I mean, the cat was really old, slept all the time, ornery as hell, but it was still sad. There was no funeral. My mom called Animal Control and they came to take her away."

"Pets fulfill us in a way," he said. "Taking care of something, or someone else, is good for the soul. It's what we're meant to do."

She thought about how she'd taken care of Roland and many of the things she'd done only to be betrayed. Sheila said, "But you've got to be loved back."

He looked at her, said, "Best case scenario, sure, but love without reciprocation is also real."

On that note they walked in silence. She wondered what he thought of her, if he was still mad for breaking it off. He hadn't brought it up and acted as if nothing had happened between them, but something told her he still carried the torch, the way he looked at her. She felt the need to explain and said, "I'm sorry it didn't work out between us, it's just ..."

"Still trying to figure out what I did wrong."

"You did nothing wrong," she said. "I wasn't in a place to be in a relationship back then. The timing wasn't right."

"I get it. You were looking for a better option. Or maybe you had one."

"I didn't know you," she said, "and I shouldn't have drank so much."

"Do you regret it?" he asked. "That we ... uhm?"

"A little."

"Yes or no?"

"I felt a little guilty."

Eddie said, "I know this might sound weird, but during the shoot on the last movie, there were things about you that really stuck with me. I couldn't help but notice how hard you worked. That's what made you really attractive."

"My work ethic?"

"No, that you were always on task, but also very cool and laid-back," he said. "I could see that you were committed but still had a sense of humor. And I have to say, you looked really great the night of the wrap party. I hardly recognized you wearing a dress. And heels."

"I borrowed those shoes from my roommate, Lisa," she confessed. "The next day I was so embarrassed. I mean ... I never sleep with anyone on the first date, and we weren't even on a date. I didn't know what you'd expect."

"We could have started over again, taken it slow."

"I guess."

"The couple of times we went out afterward, for sushi and those screenings, you had fun, right?"

"Yeah," she said.

"But I'm not really your type, am I?"

"I don't know if I have a type," she said.

"But Roland's your type."

"You know Roland?"

"From the gym. Not very well, but I've seen him around. And I saw you guys out together."

"Where?"

"Happy hour on the Third Street Promenade."

"I didn't see you."

"I made it a point not to be noticed. Maybe because I was jealous."

"So, you were stalking me?" she teased.

"No. It was random, and just a few months ago. It looked like you guys were having fun so I avoided you."

"Roland's a douchebag," she said.

Eddie laughed, said, "What?"

"Nothing."

"Why's he a douche?"

"He slept with my roommate."

"No!"

"I caught them," she said with a nod.

Eddie laughed and then apologized with, "Sorry, it's not funny."

"My soon-to-be ex-roommate is a paralegal, makes good money, has really cool style. Great clothes, great shoes. Satin sheets. Lisa's the kind of girl that gets her nails done, takes gourmet-cooking classes, and drives an Audi."

"I know the type."

"She's a girlie-girl, while I hardly put on makeup. I guess Roland's into all that. Maybe they deserve each other. I remember now, catching him looking at her a certain way. I should have seen it coming."

"Betrayed by both of them."

"Because I'm just a bottom feeder."

"Bottom feeder?" he asked.

Sheila explained her theory about those working in the entertainment industry, including herself, who are much like catfish or crawdads, surviving off refuse that sinks to the bottom.

"You mean working on movies like this?" he asked.

"Exactly."

"Now wait a minute," he said, "don't bottom feeders eat a lot of shit?"

"That's my point," she said. "It's the nature of things. The cream rises to the top while the shit rolls downhill."

Amused, Eddie said, "I guess that's true. We eat a lot of shit just to squeak out our meager existence, don't we?"

"For some reason, mine is piled especially high," she motioned with her hands as if trying to swim to the surface above her head, "and I can't get out of it."

"That's me all right," he said, "a bottom feeder. You nailed it."

"I don't plan on being one forever," she said.

"Both of us could use a career metamorphosis."

"As long as it's not Kafkaesque."

He laughed. "Okay, but scientists say cockroaches will rule the world someday."

"Probably, but not when we're around."

"Bottom feeders. I like that."

They walked for a while in silence. She couldn't believe this was happening to her. Sheila just wanted to get back to LA. It was starting to get dark by the time she saw the cabin. "Look," she said pointing.

"Tami's compound."

"A phone," Sheila said, hopeful.

CHAPTER
THIRTY

Tom was certain he heard someone coming up behind, the worrisome sound of twigs snapping, the crunch of footsteps back there somewhere in the trees. He picked up his pace.

He didn't see the sinkhole. Tom's foot sank and he stumbled. He rolled headfirst into a bed of pine needles and his hat flew off.

There was sharp pain and he knew immediately that he'd sprained his ankle. He'd done it before as a kid playing football, tripping over sprinkler heads. Through the burning discomfort, Tom got up and pressed on, without his hat.

He ducked below branches, hobbled over a brook, and cut through a meadow. When the pain was too much, he ducked behind a tree and took a break. Heart racing, sweating, he dropped down and held his ankle, now throbbing. *Son of a bitch!*

The sounds of pursuit grew closer. Someone was definitely back there.

He spotted a cluster of tall weeds in a ravine below and got an idea. He grabbed a dried branch near him, rolled over, and plopped himself into the narrow crevice. It was cool and there was enough foliage to cover him completely—a hiding place.

He pulled the fallen branch over, like a blanket, and tried to steady his breathing. He trained his ears but could only hear his own heart pounding.

Tom tried his best to stay completely still. Then he heard the footsteps. They were getting closer. At the same time, he realized he was lying in an anthill. He batted a few off his face and could feel them crawling into his collar and up his pant leg.

Tom heard the mysterious hunter stop for a moment, followed by the sound of breathing. It sounded so close he dared not move or look up. The ants were now stinging the back of his neck as he clenched his teeth, enduring the pain.

Be still. Don't move.

Finally, the footsteps continued. He listened as they moved past him. Tom considered that there might be more than one killer as he stared up through the branches at the sky beyond the treetops, waiting, enduring it all, jaw clenched as ants feasted on his sweaty flesh.

When he couldn't take it anymore, Tom rolled from his hiding place and batted away what ants he could, shaking out his shirt, taking down his pants and flicking them off his thighs. He pulled his pants back up and rolled away, finding refuge in a nearby cluster of weeds. This hiding place wasn't as good as the other, but at least it wasn't an anthill.

He heard a noise and peeked out. He could see, within the trees up ahead, a figure dressed in camouflage coming back up the hill toward him. *Shit!*

Tom ducked down and pressed his face to the dirt. He listened as the footsteps came closer, the sound of gravel shuffling and twigs snapping underfoot. He so wished he still had that Glock. *Why did I waste the bullets on that stupid dog?*

But it sounded as if the footsteps were farther away and, this time, circling around him before moving past and back up the hill.

He didn't move or even look up.

The woods fell silent, and Tom gave it a good ten minutes before he finally, cautiously, sat up. He reached into his collar and picked away the remaining ants, crushing the little bastards in his fingers.

When he felt it was safe enough to proceed, Tom stood and limped downhill, the opposite direction from where the mysterious camouflaged killer had gone. His path became steeper and the ground slippery as loose rocks slipped below his feet.

Tom reached the clearing and stopped at the edge of a deep ravine, a cliff before him—no way to proceed. His heart sank and he realized he had to turn back. He would have to retrace his steps, back where the killer had gone.

Son of a bitch.

Slowly and cautiously he made his way back up. His feet kept slipping on the loose slate, the pain in his ankle getting much worse. The steep embankment offered little foothold, so he pulled on sapling branches and exposed roots to climb back up the embankment.

Tom finally made it to level ground and limped on. He passed the crevice where he had hidden and scanned the surroundings before he hunched down among the weeds and cautiously cut through a meadow. He could smell the smoke from the fire. He had a headache—the flu symptoms were back.

Tom stopped from time to time to listen but heard nothing but birds and the soft wind rustling the pines. He reached the sinkhole he'd stepped into, the place where he'd sprained his ankle. That's when he realized something was missing—his cowboy hat.

The killer had his hat.

Shit.

CHAPTER
THIRTY-ONE

Eddie used the butt of the shotgun to break the windowpane of the French door. Careful not to cut his wrist on the jagged shards of glass, he reached in and unlocked the deadbolt. They were in.

Sheila searched the kitchen while he rummaged through the living room. There were piles of clothes and half-packed suitcases on the floor. He saw the home phone was missing from its charging stand. He pushed the locator button but heard no signal.

"Mine always ends up on the couch," Sheila said.

Eddie searched there for the wireless phone receiver, flipping over cushions. Nothing.

"Maybe there's one upstairs," Eddie said.

The master bedroom had a Western motif, with silhouettes of cowboys roping cattle hand-sewn into the quilted bedspread. There were photos from actual rodeos and decorative pillows with branding iron symbols set against the distressed-wood headboard. This was the largest room in the house and had its own master bath, so Eddie assumed this was Tami's room. He wondered what she'd thought of the room's theme, if the cattle and horses depicted on the bedspread were treated unkindly.

There was another wireless charging base on the nightstand but no phone there either. Eddie pushed that locater button but, like the one downstairs, nothing sounded.

Sheila stated the obvious, "Someone took the phones."

"Maybe our cell phones work here," Eddie said. He set the shotgun down and pulled out his iPhone. "No service," he read aloud.

"Who would take the phones?" Sheila wondered aloud.

"God knows. Maybe there's a router we can tap into for Wi-Fi," Eddie said, fingering the screen. "Wait a second. There is."

Sheila went to his side to consider his phone over his shoulder. "Is there a network?" she asked.

He could see an active network but there was a lock symbol next to the address. He pressed it but it asked for a password. "I don't know the password so I can't access the damn thing."

"This is crazy," Sheila said in frustration.

"Yeah."

As she stood close to him beside the bed, Eddie recalled the night they'd slept together. It wasn't that long ago when they both stood in his apartment beside his bed, much like they were now. He remembered they'd reached a lull in their conversation and she'd looked at him with a wry smile he'd never forget. Then she leaned in. The rest was history.

Since Sheila had initiated the intimacy that night, it confounded him that she so abruptly broke it off. Sex with him couldn't have been that bad, could it? What had gone wrong? He wanted to talk about it more but this clearly was not the time.

A rustling noise came from the closet.

Sheila flinched.

Eddie grabbed the shotgun. "Who is it?" he said.

There was silence.

They shared a look before Eddie flung the closet door open.

Tami was hiding under a pile of ski parkas. "Don't shoot!" she shrieked, squinting up at them, waving her hand, bracelets jingling.

"Tami?"

"Please don't hurt me."

"What are you doing here?" Eddie said.

"Hiding," she said, her voice cracking in fear.

"Did you see the killer?" Sheila asked her.

"No, but I heard the screams."

"What screams?"

Tami burst into tears before she managed to utter, "Connie, Bonnie, and Diane. It was horrible."

"Why aren't you down at the Gold Strike?" Eddie asked.

"The driver dropped us all off to get our things. I needed my insulin."

"But the sheriff ordered everyone to go down and gather at the Gold Strike," Sheila said.

"I don't care what that loathsome sheriff wanted, and I wasn't going to wait around in that horrible place. Not with all those dead animals. I needed my medication."

"Where's your insulin?" Sheila said. "I'll get it."

"Um ... I ..." Tami stammered.

"Is it an insulin pen? My mom had one of those so I know how to prepare them," Sheila offered. "Is it in your bag?"

"You see, it's complicated. I'm, uh ..."

"You're not a diabetic, are you?" Sheila said.

"Of course ... Um ... you see ..." Tami raised her hands as if in surrender, "Okay, I admit I'm not a diabetic. I made that up at the time." She looked to Eddie with pleading eyes, "Ed, you know I'm very sensitive. You understand."

Eddie turned to Sheila and gave her a nod, impressed she was able to root out the truth. He could see she was livid. Turning back to Tami, he asked, "Tami, why did you guys come back here?"

"I told you, to get my things. And I had no intention of waiting at the hotel."

"Do you know where the phones are?" Sheila asked.

"Phones?"

"They're missing," she said pointing to the charging stand.

"Yes, I know. I couldn't find them either. They were there before. I called my agent last night."

"Tell us what happened."

Tami heaved a heavy sigh before she said, "The plan was to pack our bags and bring them out to the road to wait for Don to come back after he dropped everyone off. I was up here packing when I heard the screams. Then I saw them running."

"Who?" asked Eddie.

"My staff."

"Where?"

"They ran off into the woods. I could see from up here. Then there were these horrendous screams …" she said, emotion returning to her voice, "That's when I hid in here. And after the screams I could hear the killer come upstairs and look for me." She sniffled, wiped tears, then continued, "He finally gave up and then I could hear him rummaging around downstairs."

"The kitchen knife," Sheila said.

Eddie said, "Let's see."

A moment later the three of them stood in the kitchen and, sure enough, the largest of the kitchen knives was missing from the wooden block. Sheila explained to Tami how they'd come across Don on the road, the knife lodged in his neck.

Tami covered her mouth with her hand and uttered, "Oh, my."

"Maybe the killer was squatting in this house," Sheila ventured.

Eddie nodded then turned to Tami. "Did anything strange happen while you were here, anything off-kilter?"

"Not that I recall."

"All the doors were locked when we got here. Did you do that?" he asked.

"No."

"You didn't lock the doors?"

"No. I hid in the closet."

"So maybe the killer has keys to the house," Sheila said.

"Let's not stick around and find out," Eddie said, eyeing the darkening sky out the window. "It's time to go."

"Where?" Tami asked.

"The Gold Strike," Eddie said and grabbed the shotgun.

"How are we going to get down there?"

"Walk," Sheila said.

Tami clearly didn't like the idea and exclaimed, "I say we wait here until someone comes for help."

Sheila said, "Nobody knows we're here."

As they turned for the door, Eddie bumped into Diane's portfolio resting on the kitchen counter. It fell onto the tile floor and popped open. Something caught his eye. Tucked inside the portfolio was a scrapbook with worn edges, its pages now open too. There was a photo of a much younger Diane, archer's bow aimed. "Wait a second," he said, and picked up the scrapbook. "Hold on a second."

"What?" Sheila asked.

Eddie scanned a newspaper article with the headline, "US Woman's Archery Takes Aim at Rio."

"She's an archer?" Eddie asked Tami.

"Who?" Sheila inquired.

"Tami's stylist, Diane."

Tami stepped up to view the scrapbook. "Archery?"

"It looks like she competed in the Olympics." Eddie flipped the pages to more newspaper articles.

"She never told me that."

There were photos of Diane in competition, images of women in the archer stance, arrows tightly grouped on targets, and even a photo of Diane as a child wearing full camo kneeling next to a man that appeared to be her father. A slain wild boar lay between them, arrows protruding. Both father and daughter held compound hunting bows.

"Oh, my …" Tami said.

"How long has Diane worked for you?" Sheila asked.

"You don't think that—?"

"Did she bring a bow up here?" asked Eddie.

"Come to think of it," Tami said in a worried tone, "Diane did have a lot of extra cases in the makeup trailer."

"What kind of cases?" Sheila pressed.

"Black ones. Like the ones the guys use for the cameras and such."

"The guys?" Sheila said.

"I mean *you* guys."

"Pelican cases?" Sheila asked.

"I suppose."

"Were they long enough to carry a bow?" Eddie asked, arms stretched out to demonstrate the size.

"I'm not sure … but I think so. No, it can't be Diane. I *know* her and there's no way she'd hurt a fly."

"Did she bring camouflage?" Eddie asked.

"Camouflage what?"

"Clothing, pants, pullovers."

Tami scoffed, "I assure you that's *not* Diane's style."

Eddie turned more pages to reveal images of Diane in competition, plus a few of her holding trophies. On the last page, there were newspaper articles with photos of her and three women standing in front of the iconic Olympic rings.

"Her Olympic teammates," Sheila said, scanning the text.

Tami started on, "I highly doubt that Diane would—"

"Wait a minute," Sheila said upon closer inspection. "These are all obits."

"Excuse me?"

"They're obituaries."

"Obituaries for who?" asked Eddie.

Sheila read one for a second more then turned to him and said, "Her other Olympic teammates. All three of them ... murdered."

CHAPTER
THIRTY-TWO

Tom felt light-headed as he scanned the trees for signs of an ambush. He weighed either proceeding or staying where he was. Then *the wave* hit, just as it had when he first arrived at the Gold Strike, one of the dreadful sudden panic attacks he couldn't control. He fought it off the best he could, but the anxiety was too great. He felt dizzy.

He sat on a tree stump to let it pass, closed his eyes and tried to put himself somewhere else, anywhere but here. He tried to imagine the blue ocean, like in an acting-class exercise, but the pain in his ankle was the ball and chain that kept tugging Tom's mind back to the here and now. The throbbing ache was getting worse. He slapped away another ant still crawling on his neck.

After a few minutes, the disorienting feeling passed and Tom stood and steadied himself. It appeared safe. He figured the killer must have found his hat and then come down the hill to the cliff to look for him before turning back. But there's only one way out of here, he realized, back up the hill. *The killer must know that.*

Tom trained his ears for any sign of movement. There was nothing. When he felt it was safe, he decided to proceed and pushed through the discomfort to hobble on. The swelling ankle made his movement slow. It was getting dark.

Tom made it another one hundred feet or so when he sensed someone up ahead. He stopped in his tracks. That's when he saw her. Dressed head to toe in dark-green camouflage, Diane stood in his path. She appeared relaxed, leaning against a tree, a hunter's bow at her side. The weapon looked so strange to him, like it was out of a science fiction movie; a high-tech web of support struts, the bow's string pulled tight around cams and pulleys on each end. It too was painted camouflage. This was not the same weapon he'd seen in movies like *Rambo* or *The Hunger Games*, no, this bow appeared to be a precision tool of some kind, sinister and deadly.

His cowboy hat lay at her feet.

"Diane?" he said, heart racing.

"Diana," she corrected him.

Tom was amazed at how seamlessly she blended into the surroundings. Branches and foliage were stuck in the netting of her vest, much like military snipers he'd seen on TV. With that and the impromptu tree perch she'd fashioned back at base camp, *no wonder why nobody saw her.*

"Diana, not Diane … it's Diana," she said firmly. "That's who I am."

"Oh, sorry, I thought—"

"The goddess of the hunt." It was as if she spoke with another voice, as another persona.

"Excuse me?" he said.

"The hunt."

"Diana. Got it. No problem," he said. "Why are you …?" he started in but trailed off, not wanting to make her angry.

"We stand in the garden of the oaks, a sacred place," she lectured, motioning to the trees surrounding them. "Home of Earth's beautiful creatures."

There was something in her eyes Tom could see, a burning

hatred and anger. He took a few deep breaths, eyes still locked on Diane, and asked, "Why are you doing this?"

"I protect the animals. And you have crossed me. You have sinned." She reached back to pull an arrow from the quiver strapped to her back.

"Diane. I mean Diana … hold on a second. I won't say a word to anyone, I swear to God. This shit is none of my business. I'm just an actor for Chrissake."

She studied him silently as she thumbed the flight of her arrow into the bow's taut string.

"Look, I'll tell you what," Tom tried to reason, "This can be our secret. I didn't see you, you didn't see me. Deal? And I won't say a word, ever, to anyone. I swear to God. Let's just go home and—"

"What about that defenseless dog?" she said as she raised the bow. "Why did you have to kill it?"

"That mongrel was attacking me, and I—"

She let the arrow fly.

The sudden jolt surprised him.

Tom could see the shaft protruding from his chest. He could feel the arrowhead end sticking out of his middle-back, realized, *It went right through me.* His neck stiffened and his hands curled inward. His knees gave way and he dropped. Gasping for air, Tom could feel his heart clench. *Bitch shot me!* The pain became overwhelming. *Because of a fucking dog!*

He couldn't breathe. It was as if the wind were knocked out of him and as much as he tried he couldn't draw a breath. Blood began to fill his throat, salty to taste, and he saw Diane come up to him. He felt her foot on his chest before she yanked the arrow out. There was an explosion of pain as the retraction of the arrow pulled him up off the dirt.

With his hands, he tried to cover the puncture wound to stop the bleeding.

Diane stepped up into Tom's view. She stared down at him, a

look of disgust on her face. "How's it feel now, big man?"

Tom was finally able to draw short breaths but only from hyper-ventilating. Diane stepped away and out of his view. He wondered where she was going—*for another arrow*? He craned his neck but couldn't see.

Beyond the tips of the trees Tom focused on a single star in the dusky cobalt sky.

God help me.

There were burning embers floating above, like floating fireflies, ash from the burning trees as the fire spread like cancer. Then smoke from the fires drifted in and clouded his view of the heavens above.

With all his might, he fought off death, an icy coldness climbing up his spine. He felt Diane's presence above him, and he could see she was fiddling with something as she put on some kind of headgear. It was a monocle scope-like device. Over one eye she adjusted a nob on its side.

Tom recognized it as night-vision goggles.

When she was satisfied, Diane flipped up the monocle scope, stepped over, and stared down at him once again. She spit on him, then said, "Pathetic little man," before she walked off into the trees.

Tom closed his eyes and finally was able to transport himself to somewhere else. He now stood in the wings of the Ensemble Theatre of Cincinnati and was about to make the stage entrance of his much-celebrated run of Shakespeare's *Richard III*. This was *his* moment. A stagehand, a beautiful redhead, smiled at him and made last-minute adjustments to his wardrobe as he waited for his cue.

They'll love me.

The footlights dimmed and he stepped out onto the boards.

Darkness engulfed.

CHAPTER
THIRTY-THREE

Diane marched down the hill. The *voice* was back in her head and now it was repeating, "*Kill them, kill them all.*"

The *voice* said so.

Obey.

That stupid actor. He didn't need to shoot the dog. He got what he deserved. And this entire production, everyone up here, is guilty of killing that poor horse. Yet another example of innocent animals being enslaved and exploited for human amusement.

Kill them all.

She didn't intend things to go from bad to worse, but they had. Last night, the day the horse was euthanized, and after all were asleep, the *voice* came back to her. She could never sleep when she heard it in her head. The *voice* said to sneak out of the cabin and free the other horses, so she obeyed.

It was a full moon, so she didn't need a flashlight as she made the long trek up the hill. Up on set there was a light in one of the trailers. She snuck up to discover a security guard asleep inside.

At the stable, Jimmy the cowboy was there, and drunk. Patches' death was his fault, and she hated him with every ounce of her soul. This was the man who made a living out of exploiting these poor animals. Her bow was hidden in Tami's trailer, so she quietly retrieved it.

Before she came up to the mountains, she'd had her bow restrung but hadn't tested it yet. While setting up Tami's trailer the other day, she'd found the opportunity and snuck away. Diane was surprised how much added power the new strings brought, so much so that, in testing the new tension, she'd aimed at a tree but missed. The arrow instead got loose and hit the camera truck a hundred yards away. Oops. So she packed her bow away and hid it all in Tami's trailer.

She'd returned to the stable and made the cowboy pay for his sins, but unfortunately, as she went for another arrow, he got away. Diane searched all around but couldn't find him. He hadn't gone to the security guard. Diane checked and the fat guy was still asleep and snoring, hadn't moved an inch.

She was certain she'd hit Jimmy in the face, knew he wouldn't get far so where could he have gone? She attempted to free the other horses, but they wouldn't move. As much as she tried to scoot them out of the barn they were content to just stand there, looking at her. Didn't they realize they were now free?

Covering her tracks, Diane pulled her bow and arrows out of the trailer and hid them, along with all her cases and camouflage, tucked away back in the trees. That way when they found Jimmy they couldn't connect it to her.

She returned to her cabin that night figuring eventually someone from the crew would find Jimmy, but strangely there was no mention of it next day, not until Tami discovered Jimmy's body on the floor of the stagecoach. That's when Diane realized he'd hidden there. No wonder she couldn't find him.

But now the forest was afire and destroying God's creatures, all because of that chain-smoking asshole. But she'd taken care of him. He got what he deserved.

It all started to come apart when Tami convinced Don to drop them off at the cabin so she could get their things. Had Stuart been on the shuttle, Don wouldn't have agreed, but Tami was the star of the film and got her way. The plan was to bring their bags out to the road so he could pick them up on the next run down.

Diane liked the idea of getting out of there. She'd go back to LA and wait until everything died down before going back for her hidden bow and arrows.

But then the *voice* came. It told her what to do. Now the sinners would "*know how it feels to be the hunted one.*"

"Okay, okay," she replied aloud, talking back to the *voice*. "I'll do it, I'll do it, I'll do it."

"Do what?" Connie said.

She and Bonnie had heard her.

"Who are you talking to?" Connie asked.

"Nobody."

"You were talking to someone."

"No, I wasn't."

"Yes, you were. We heard you. Are you all right?"

Diane had been talking back to the *voice* more and more now and it was getting harder to hide it in public. When she couldn't help it, Diane used earbuds and held her cell phone in hand to fake she was in conversation. That worked most of the time and nobody had thought she talked to herself. But it didn't work in front of Connie and Bonnie that afternoon.

They glared at her.

As a teenager she'd heard the *voice* from time to time, but that was only in a sleep state, half in and half out of consciousness. And those were just whispers. It was in Rio, the day before the Olympic match, that's when the *voice* came in loud and clear, and it wouldn't stop.

She hadn't told her coaches or teammates about it because they'd think it was weird. Who wouldn't? She hadn't slept the night before the team event against the Koreans. Diane couldn't make the *voice* in her head stop that day, and she fell apart. It became obvious her performance was the sole reason why Team USA didn't advance to the finals for a chance at a medal. They'd have to wait another four years. Most, if not all of them, would be replaced by younger archers on the circuit, all because of the *voice*.

Then those bitches on her team shamed her, some directly and vocally, others just by the looks they gave her. Diane was the weak link. She'd smashed all their Olympic dreams.

The *voice* said to kill them. Diane obeyed.

She'd planned it carefully, waited until they were back home, months later and after it all had blown over. She stalked each of them, one by one. Her plan was to make each death look like either an accident or a suicide. Diane followed them from afar, took notes, and figured out each of their daily routines. Then, when the time was right, she drew each one out to places where they'd be alone. The best part was the look in their eyes when her teammates realized *she* was killing them. That was the best. It made Diane feel powerful. *If they'd just kept their mouths shut.*

But she hadn't counted on all that blood.

Logic told her the police would not think it a mere coincidence that three of the four women of the US Olympic Archery Team had all come to a sudden, violent death. The cops would come to her, the only surviving team member. They'd ask where she'd been. They'd track her cell phone and have surveillance video of her coming and going. She'd seen enough detective shows to know what to do. It was time to disappear.

Diane had to reinvent herself and take on a new persona. She decided it would be the goddess Diana, the beautiful one holding the bow, the protector of nature and animals. She'd always been drawn to the Roman goddess depicted in statues and paintings. The gilded one at the Philadelphia Museum of Art was her all-time favorite. She'd learned this famous Augustus Saint-Gaudens statue had once stood atop Madison Square Garden in New York—not the stadium where the Knicks play now, but the original building that was torn down long ago. She loved that Diana's symbols were the moon, water, forest, and sun, all things she adored, plus since her name was so close—it made sense. It was meant to be.

And what better place to reinvent yourself than Hollywood?

She gathered as much money as she could, emptying her bank account, selling her jewelry and most of her things with the exception of two bows: her prized tournament bow, a delicate instrument designed for the archery range, and the weapon her father gave her; the most powerful bow known to man, the rugged PSE Full Throttle—deadly accuracy at over 370 feet per second. There were also all those hunting arrows with the razor-sharp mechanical broadheads. Dad had bought so many of those things.

As a child, it was her father who taught Diane how to shoot and hunt. This was the "quality time" father and daughter spent together, traipsing through the woods at the crack of dawn. He'd taught her everything, how to shoot, sneak up on prey, how to camouflage and appear invisible.

He taught her about guns too. Hunting became their favorite pastime.

But then, as a teenager, Diane woke up one morning and couldn't hunt anymore. She realized it made her sad to watch as these animals suffered. It felt so wrong, so cruel. She loved nature too much. "Why do we need to kill them?" she asked her father. He didn't have an answer.

In tears, as they were about to set out one morning, she told her father she couldn't hunt anymore.

He was disappointed, she could tell. Dad chalked it off as her blossoming maternal instinct, calling it a "female thing." He said if she were a boy she wouldn't have these same feelings. Diane wondered if that were true.

To keep her father happy, Diane continued with archery, but with targets instead of living things. So her father overcompensated.

He built an archery range in the backyard and bought the very best competition bows. He hired coaches and drove her around the country from tournament to tournament. She practiced every day after school, often until her fingers bled. Diane excelled in the sport and filled her room with trophies and plaques.

They called her a natural.

Archery soon defined her—first a college scholarship, then Olympic Team USA. But then, as they waited for Rio, her father had the heart attack. All of a sudden, he was gone.

Diane had wondered at the time why she didn't feel anything.

At the funeral she pretended to be sad for the benefit of others, but deep down inside there was nothing there. She thought maybe the heart attack was dad's karma for slaughtering all those innocent animals. Maybe nature had simply taken its course.

At first, she was disappointed that her dad would never see his daughter compete in the Olympics, but then she realized she didn't have to prove herself to anyone anymore.

That seemed like so long ago.

Another life.

On Diane's drive out to Los Angeles, she imagined her Ford Explorer a virtual cocoon. She'd go in the car a fuzzy, ugly worm and emerge a beautiful butterfly. Rebirth.

She found a sublet apartment in Studio City and looked for gainful employment. On the internet, she searched for news that the Olympic Team had been murdered and one of them was missing. These news reports only fueled her. She stole a portfolio from a costume designer and lied that the work was hers. She colored her hair and gave herself a complete makeover. She spent countless hours running, working out, getting stronger. Occasionally she'd drive into the mountains or desert to be alone. There she'd practice her archery.

After she successfully reinvented herself in Los Angeles, Diane attended an Animal Stance charity event. That's where she met

Tami, and the actress hired Diane to rebrand her flailing image. At first Diane was ecstatic, but it didn't take long before she couldn't stand Tami. *Such a demanding bitch!* Diane soon found herself picking up Tami's dry cleaning and running stupid errands, the kind of stuff a personal assistant does, not a professional brand consultant. Diane was livid and would have quit but she needed the money. Plus, the situation worked to conceal her. Tami paid Diane through her nonprofit like a vendor, with no payroll service or background check to discover Diane was using a false last name and bogus Social Security number.

Oh sure, Tami said that she cared for animal welfare but it was always about *her*, always *her*. Diane came to realize Animal Stance was all a ruse, all part of Tami's supposed brand, a nonprofit cause the actress could hang her hat on to prop up her image, as if she cared.

Since Tami was on such a restrictive diet, it was Diane's job to do the reconnaissance for Tami's needs once it was established they'd be shooting up in the mountains. Tami demanded all of her meals were vegan and strictly organic. It's easy to get that stuff in Los Angeles with plenty of Whole Foods and Bristol Farms stores around, but try finding those places in blue-collar San Bernardino County. Diane called around and searched the internet. She found one store down in Upland, but the drive between there and set would be too long. The solution was for her to scout the handful of tiny mom-and-pop organic markets near the movie ranch. Diane made a day out of it and set out in her Ford Explorer. She'd found one place that looked promising, overpriced, but the produce looked good. It was still a drive from the shooting location but at least it wasn't all the way down the mountain.

Diane was scouting for other options when she came across that fat asshole who hit the deer. She watched in horror as the guy crushed the animal's skull with that rock. It brought back memories of her father putting innocent deer and wild boars out of their misery, so brutal. Although the *voice* didn't talk to her to that afternoon, Diane killed the bastard anyway, and used that same big rock to finish the job. *Fucker deserved it.*

Again, it made her feel powerful.

And it gave her peace.

"Are you all right?" Bonnie asked again as they packed their bags. "You were talking to someone."

"It's nothing," Diane replied. "I just—"

"What's this?" Connie said when she discovered Diane's scrapbook. Diane snatched it back and told her to mind her own business.

"They know," the *voice* said to Diane.

Although she didn't have the bow and arrows down at the cabin, she found a way to take care of Connie and Bonnie with a kitchen knife. Then she went for Tami, but somehow in the confusion the actress got away and Diane couldn't find her. She didn't want Tami to call for help, so she took the phones from the house and went out looking for her. Don returned in the van. She tossed the phones in the trees and told him that the others weren't ready yet but she needed to get something from Tami's trailer. She saw him hide his cigarettes when she got in the van. As they went back to get the last of the cast and crew, that's when she took care of the careless bastard that started the fire.

She went to get the bow and arrows she'd stashed. The *voice* told her what she had to do.

Diane was methodical, just like the mornings hunting with her dad. First, she took care of the annoying deputy, then that punk from the camera department, the Eurotrash cinematographer, and then that old man that showed up. It felt great. But the others found guns which made things complicated.

Diane terrorized them, tried to burn them out of the trailer but they got away and then split up. She followed the one that killed the dog and took care of him.

Now, Diane ran back to take care of the rest of them and

cover the last of her tracks. It was dark by the time she got to the movie ranch. She could see the fire had reached the Western sets, with its eerie glow and dancing shadows, the smoke making her cough. Burning embers floated above the treetops, spreading the fire to God knows where. She could see the trailer she'd set afire had burned completely, now smoldering. The camera truck would surely go up next.

Where are the others?

Armed with her trusty bow, wearing her dad's night-vision goggles, the goddess of the hunt pressed on.

CHAPTER THIRTY-FOUR

Sheila led the way as they set out from the cabin. Tami and Eddie behind her, they pushed through the brush making their own path down the mountain.

Tami broke the silence. "Maybe it's all a coincidence."

"What?" Eddie asked.

"That Diane's Olympic teammates are all dead."

Sheila said, "Those obituaries read like they were murdered."

"Okay … but maybe this killer could be tracking Diane right now, terrorizing all of us. I mean, I just have a hard time believing that—"

"Shh!" Sheila said. She saw the body up ahead, recognized the sweater and realized it was Connie. Tami saw her too and gasped. Eddie brushed past them and approached.

"Throat cut," Eddie said. He leaned down and held Connie's wrist to check her pulse.

A shaken Tami said, "Then Bonnie must be around here somewhere."

"Maybe she got away," Sheila said.

"Yes, maybe she went for help," Tami said with hope, looking out into the trees.

Eddie said, "Diane must have chased her from the house and then slashed her throat with that kitchen knife."

"The knife we found in Don," Sheila said with a nod.

"That's right."

"I still can't believe Diane would do this," Tami said.

Sheila was tired of Tami's denial, said, "You heard them screaming. Did you hear Diane? Was she ever in distress?"

"I can't remember," Tami said.

"Yes or no?"

"I don't know."

"Think. What did you hear?"

"It may have only been Connie and Bonnie."

"Then it has to be her."

"But why would she do it?" Tami questioned. "We were only nice to her. All of us."

"You know her better than anyone," Eddie said. "Why would she?"

Tami was at a loss.

"We should keep moving," Sheila said.

As they proceeded through the trees, Tami continued her lament, "I just can't believe Diane would do something so horrible. She seemed so professional, so self-assured." Tami explained how she'd met Diane at an animal welfare charity event and that after they'd gotten to know each other Diane proposed that Tami hire her as a consultant to rebrand Tami's image. They'd hired photographers and a savvy publicist to place her at locations where the paparazzi were known to lurk. "And it was working," Tami said. "After all these years I'm back in the magazines and in social media."

Eddie recalled, "I remember seeing you on TMZ waiting for your bags at the airport."

"Yes, that was one of those times. I wasn't really on a flight that day," Tami confessed.

"What do you mean?" asked Eddie.

"Diane put me in a wonderful ensemble, very chic. She even found designer luggage to match, everything perfect. We got a limo and I waited at baggage claim, made it look like I was coming in from New York."

"It was all fake?"

"It was real except I wasn't arriving on a flight that day. I don't know if you remember, but the questions those TMZ reporters asked me were absolutely ridiculous, and vulgar, but I guess that's the point of that show, isn't it?"

Sheila asked, "Did Diane ever behave strangely?"

"Not really, but she's very opinionated," Tami said. "Sure, we had creative differences, but she would eventually come around to seeing it my way."

"Nothing out of the ordinary?" Sheila inquired.

"I caught her talking to herself."

"What do you mean?"

"She was talking to someone, but there was nobody there. The funny thing is once she saw me she pretended to be on her cell phone and pulled out earbuds."

"Was she ever violent?" Sheila asked.

"Heavens no."

As they proceeded down the hill, Tami increasingly slowed their progress. This bothered Sheila. "You have to keep up," she urged.

"I'm sorry, I'm trying," Tami said. "It's these shoes."

Sheila glanced down at the thin flip-flops on Tami's feet. "Don't you have anything better than that?"

"Back in the cabin," she said pointing up the hill.

"What were you thinking?" Sheila said in frustration.

"I have boots in my bag, and running shoes, Skechers."

"We're not going back," Sheila said.

"It won't take long, and I can—"

"We're not going back," Sheila pressed. "Just keep up with us. And keep quiet."

Tami's tone turned defiant. "I will *not* be spoken to like this." Tami turned to Eddie and with a wave of her hand said, "Ed, please get a handle on your staff. I won't stand for her insolence."

"Insolence?!" Sheila said. "Face it, Tami, this is *all* your fault. You had to have your own people to pamper you and make you feel good about yourself. Just so happens one of them is a crazy, murderous bitch."

"Preposterous," Tami said.

"How ridiculous is the size of your trailer," Sheila continued, getting it off her chest, "and that you have three people at your beck and call, like it's going to make a difference? All the time and effort that goes into that bullshit ... Face it, Tami, you're incredibly self-centered and couldn't give a shit about anyone else."

"Ladies!" Eddie said, trying to make peace.

"I'll have you know," Tami countered, "on my series, the network—"

"This isn't your fucking series!" Sheila snapped back. "Those days are long gone. This is a low-budget cable TV quickie piece of shit nobody's going to see. The Majestic Channel? That's a network for old geezers."

"Sheila," Eddie said, trying to calm her down.

A defiant Tami said, "I won't stand here and—"

"Production rents you your own cabin," Shelia cut her off, "and meanwhile the camera department goes without prime lenses?"

"I have no idea what you are talking about," Tami said, back on her heels.

"Face it. Your crazy-ass stylist is a killer," Sheila said. "And now you're slowing us down with your spa footwear."

"I had no idea that we—"

"Sshh!" Eddie hushed. "Listen."

They all trained their ears. It sounded like a vehicle was approaching on the dirt road.

"What is it?" Tami asked.

"Sounds like a car," said Eddie.

Tami gave Sheila a dismissive sneer before she said, "Thank God. Get me out of here." With that Tami began to navigate her way out of the trees.

But Sheila sensed something was not right. From the way the headlights reflected off the trees, it appeared the car was approaching from above, not below. Before she could say anything, Tami had emerged from the trees. She ran out onto the middle of the dirt road.

Sheila could see the jerky guy's pickup round the bend.

Tami, now in the truck's headlights, waved her arms and screamed, "Help!"

The truck slowed at the top of the hill as if assessing the situation. It turned on its high beams.

"Please help us!" Tami shouted, arms waving, the sound of her bracelets jingling. She began striding up the road toward the truck.

The engine revved.

"Tami, no!" Eddie shouted. He ran for her.

Sheila could see the expression on Tami's face, utter confusion as to why the pickup was accelerating and coming right at her. Then the realization hit Tami. She dropped her arms and tried to scramble off the road. No luck. Her flip-flops on the loose dirt gained little traction.

The truck hit hard.

There was a loud thud and the impact sent Tami airborne. She was thrown out onto the road. The pickup rolled straight over her. Tami gave a blood-curdling scream.

Sheila stood frozen as the vehicle lurched over Tami's body. It slid to a stop, Tami squirming in the dirt behind the pickup.

White reverse lights came on illuminating the cloud of dust

in the truck's wake. The pickup backed up and rolled over the screaming Tami again, rear tires spewing dirt and gravel.

Eddie raised the shotgun and fired. It blew out the camper shell window. He pumped another round, ran up, and fired again.

The white reverse lights cut off and the truck plowed over Tami yet again.

Eddie's next shotgun blast ripped off the side-view mirror. The truck was getting away. It went over the embankment and was gone.

Sheila and Eddie both went for Tami.

One of Tami's arms was bent back over her head and her collarbone stuck out grotesquely, the white of the bone visible. Sheila could see tire tracks on Tami's face. Blood seeped out of her ears. She quivered in violent convulsions. Sheila had seen seizures like this before, on her mother's deathbed.

"Tami, hold on," Eddie said, clearly shaken.

Her eyes did not acknowledge either of them. She was off in a distant place. Then Tami's eyes found Sheila with a look of confusion before she muttered, "Don't let me die."

Sheila felt incredibly guilty that she'd been berating Tami only moments ago. *Why did she run out into the road?* She could see from the changing color in Tami's skin tone that death was knocking on the door.

First she heard it, and then she saw the truck, now turned around, pull over the rise. It came to a stop facing them. The head-lights lit both she and Eddie from a distance.

"Shit," Eddie said.

"Run!" Sheila said and abandoned Tami. She went for the cover of the trees. She looked back but Eddie did not follow. Instead he stood in defiance, shotgun raised.

"Come on!" Sheila screamed.

Diane emerged from the truck with a lever-action rifle. Sheila remembered the jerky guy mentioning that he had a Winchester .30-30, like from the TV show *The Rifleman*, and asked if he could bring it to set. That gun must have been in his truck. Diane must have found it.

Diane fired at them and Eddie returned fire with the shotgun.

There was a deafening volley of gunfire back and forth before Eddie was out of ammunition, the shotgun spent.

Sheila cold see Diane cock the lever-action rifle and advance.

Eddie ran the other direction, across the road, opposite from Sheila and out of the beam of the headlights. Sheila could see him take cover in the trees.

Diane went back to the cab and pulled out her bow. She slung it over her shoulder and placed on her head what appeared to be headgear of some kind. She adjusted a monocular device over one eye then raised the rifle again. But this time Diane pointed the gun at Sheila.

The first shot sounded and splintered a branch over her head.

Sheila turned and ran.

She heard the shot and felt a sudden jolt, a sharp pain—as if the tip of a jagged, red-hot steel pipe was jabbed into her back.

Sheila knew she'd been hit and went down hard.

CHAPTER
THIRTY-FIVE

Eddie saw Diane, backlit by the truck's headlights, wearing night-vision goggles, bow slung over her back. She carried the rifle, pointing it to fire again, and marched up the road before she veered into the trees.

He knew she was going for Sheila.

Eddie crossed the road, spent shotgun in hand, and could see a glimmer of light in the woods. With her back to him, Diane was standing over Sheila, rifle pointed.

"That was Tami," Sheila said to her.

Diane replied, "Do you have any idea what a demanding bitch she was? I gave her great advice but did she listen to me? No. Pearls to swine."

"Why are you doing this?" Sheila said in a pained voice.

"I protect those who can't protect themselves."

"Who?"

"The animals."

"What animals?"

"That horse, dog, this fire!" Diane said.

"But I didn't—"

"You movie people are so wrapped up in yourselves. It makes me sick."

Eddie drew closer. Diane's back was to him. He held the shotgun from the barrel, like a baseball bat.

Sheila said, "We saw the obituaries … your Olympic team."

"Oh, you saw that? They deserved it. All of them. They all blamed me and made my life a living hell. *She* told me to do it."

"Who?"

"The deity's voice," Diane said.

"What deity?"

"The goddess Diana. She speaks to me," she said with pride. "Only me."

Eddie swung the butt of the shotgun. The hollow crack of bone sounded. Diane's headgear flew off and she collapsed in a heap.

He grabbed the fallen Winchester. Eddie wondered if she was dead or just knocked out cold. He nudged her with his foot to make sure she wouldn't get up. There was no response.

"Shit," Sheila said, relieved.

He asked, "You all right?"

"I've been hit," Sheila said through clenched teeth, rolling on her side and trying to get up.

"Don't move." He kneeled down to take a look. Although it was dark, Eddie could see the puncture wound below her shoulder blade. Blood seeped through the cloth of her fleece pullover. "Let's get the hell out of here," he said. "Can you stand?"

"I don't know," she said in tears.

"Put your arm around my shoulder. I'll carry you."

She hooked her arm around his neck and Eddie picked her up in a bridal carry. She wasn't too heavy. He could manage. Eddie could feel she was shivering and suspected she'd gone into shock.

He marched Sheila out of the trees.

The door of the pickup was still open, the cabin lights on. He set her down where she could steady herself against the body of the truck. Aided by the light in the cab, Eddie examined the wound. "It's bleeding, but not too much," he said, trying to sound positive. "One second." There was a roll of paper towels on the floor of the truck. He blotted the wound the best he could. "Does it hurt?" he asked.

"Yes," she said, stifling tears.

"You're going to be all right," he said trying to keep her from worrying. *Stay positive.* The white paper towels soaked up the blood that blossomed—a poor man's gauze to congeal the wound. He looked for keys in the ignition but they weren't there. "The keys, she must have them," he said.

"Here we go again," she said, voice trembling.

"I'll be right back."

"Hurry."

He grabbed the Winchester and followed the path back to Diane. Eddie searched the trees but could not find her. The darkness didn't help, and it all looked the same. He lost his place.

Eddie doubled back and retraced his steps.

Something gleaming in the dirt caught his eye. He approached to see the spent shotgun lying in the spot where he had dropped it.

In the weeds was the impression of Diane's fallen body.

She was gone.

CHAPTER THIRTY-SIX

Sheila tried to control her breathing like she'd learned in yoga class but had little luck. She could feel the blood on the skin on her lower back cooling and she started shivering. Her teeth chattered.

Eddie came back, out of breath, and said, "She's not there."

"What? Where'd she go?"

"I don't know, but we've got the gun."

"She's got the bow and night-vision goggles," Sheila said then cowered back into the cab of the truck, an attempt to take cover. Diane could be anywhere.

"But she's also got one hell of a headache," Eddie said as he rummaged through the cab. He pulled the visors down, checked the glove compartment, and dug under the seats.

"Can't we just coast this thing down?" Sheila asked.

"I wish, but the steering wheel is locked. I'll carry you down."

"I'm too heavy."

"I'll manage."

"Shit," Sheila said through tears. "I'm going bleed to death, like Luther and Giovanni."

"No, you won't," he said. "Don't think like that." He slung the rifle over this shoulder and adjusted the strap. "Let's go. Put your arm around my neck."

After wiping tears on her sleeve, she did as instructed. Just as he had before, Eddie picked her up in a bridal carry. "Anything hurt?" he asked.

The wound hurt like hell but she said, "I'm okay."

"Tell me if it does."

For the first few steps she could feel him struggle under her weight. Then he found his balance and they moved down the hill. She wasn't sure how far they'd make it but figured getting away from the pickup truck was probably a good idea. Diane had the keys. She'd come back.

His body warmth suppressed her shivers. She wondered how far he could carry her. She knew the Gold Strike was still far away. The pace of his breathing increased. Sheila could smell him and thought about the night they'd spent together. She remembered how awkward he was and how uncomfortable he appeared to be the next morning, nervous and unsure about himself. But now here he was, in complete control, and saving her life.

"Thank you," she said.

"You're going to be all right," he said.

She hoped so.

As they made their way down, his breathing grew more and more labored. After a while he set her down to rest his arms. Knees weak, she leaned against him for support. She could see the front of his shirt was stained with her blood.

As he caught his breath, Eddie asked, "What was all that shit about voices in her head?"

"I think she was referring to the goddess Diana from Roman mythology."

"Mythology?"

"I remember it from a class I took in college," she said. "Diana the Huntress was always depicted with a bow."

"Like Mother Nature?"

"Sort of, but different. Diana is a stunning beauty, and really strong. It's also Wonder Woman's first name.

"Diana?"

"Yeah, and I think there's a form of witchcraft named after her."

"Witchcraft?"

"Dianic Wicca … something like that."

"Occult shit totally freaks me out. How do you know so much about this?"

She could see this made him uncomfortable. "I don't know. I just do."

Eddie said, "Witchcraft, Ouija boards, demonic clowns, all that crap freaks me out."

"It's schizophrenia, not black magic," she explained. "Voices in her head, and maybe hallucinations … they aren't things schizophrenics can control without being on medication."

He tilted his head, gave her a smile, and said, "What makes you the expert?"

Sheila explained, "I started out as a psych major then switched to art history."

"Oh? That explains it."

"But I had to drop out of college when Mom got sick."

"To take care of her?"

"The expense of the assisted-living place was the end of my college education. That's when I came to LA."

"Do you regret it?"

"It is what it is."

Eddie glanced back over his shoulder before he said, "Let's keep moving." He picked her up again and they proceeded downhill. After a moment, trying to lighten the mood, he said, "I didn't learn anything about schizophrenia in film school, but I've dated a few actresses that were totally schizo, that's for damn sure. Got lots of experience there."

"Actresses?"

"Waitresses really, but in LA ... more often than not they're an AMW."

"What's that?"

"The acronym for *actress, model, whatever.*"

"Charming."

Eddie continued, "The trick is to convince the waitress to give me her phone number, but I've never had much luck in that department. Probably should have played the guitar or been a stockbroker with a closet full of Armanis." He set her down again and continued with, "The depressing part isn't the rejection, it's the being lonely part." Eddie caught his breath, gave her a smile and picked her up again.

As they continued through the trees, she remained silent, figuring it best not engage him in conversation so he could find rhythm in his breathing. She could tell he was pushing through pain, enduring it. When exertion won out, he set her down again. By now his pants were soaked in her blood.

"You okay?" she asked.

"I'm good," he said with an unconvincing nod.

"Maybe I can walk for a bit." She tried but lost her balance.

He caught her. "If you walk, your heart rate will speed the bleeding."

"You learn that in film school?"

"Boy Scouts. Look, I'll be all right. I just need short breaks once in a while, no biggie." He reached into his pocket and checked his cell phone, said, "Still no service."

"I bet the fire took out the cell phone towers."

"Or maybe those heartless bastards at AT&T cut me off because I forgot to pay my bill."

"Seriously?"

He shook his head. "Joking. Let's go." He picked her up. Sheila locked her arms around his neck and they again continued downhill.

She doubted that Roland would have gone through all this trouble. Roland was the kind of guy who never opened a door for her and made her carry her own luggage when they traveled. Chivalry was dead in him, or never there to begin with. She accepted it then but now she hated him for it, hated that he was so self-centered.

Her adrenaline spent, Sheila was getting tired. She yawned and buried her head in his chest.

Something stopped Eddie and he set her down again.

"What is it?" she asked, leaning on a tree for support.

"Bonnie."

Sheila steadied herself on a tree and could see Bonnie sitting upright against a stump, as if she'd sat down for a rest. Her eyes were wide open and she had a perplexed look on her face. Eddie kneeled down to examine.

"She alive?" Sheila asked.

"Doesn't look like it."

"She made it far, didn't she?"

"So maybe … Diane carved up Connie and Bonnie before she went out to the road, then Don picked her up when he was coming back for us and that's when she slashed him. But Bonnie wasn't dead, so …"

Sheila finished his thought, "She made her way downhill but eventually bled out."

"Apparently so."

Sheila wondered if this would be her fate, to bleed out and die with her eyes wide open and a look of total loss and despair on her face. She averted her gaze, trying not to think about it. The shivers returned and she felt incredibly thirsty. Eddie was in the midst of picking her up again when she heard the distant noise and trained her ear.

"A car," she said.

Eddie pulled the rifle from his back, ready for battle. The sound of the engine grew louder and it became apparent that the vehicle was much larger than a common pickup, and it was coming from below. Bright headlights illuminated the road before a fire truck appeared.

Eddie ran from the trees and yelled, "Help!" but the fire truck sped past, not seeing him. He hoisted the rifle on the air and fired, levered the weapon, and fired again but the truck continued up the hill without stopping. "Shit!" he screamed in frustration before the truck disappeared from view.

"They must have not heard it," Sheila said as he returned.

"Probably had radio headsets on or something."

"They'll find the bodies and send for help."

"Unless she kills them too."

She could see him fumble with the rifle. "What?" she asked.

"Out of bullets," he said.

Sheila felt suddenly light-headed and had to sit down. Her eyelids grew more and more heavy and she really wanted to take a nap. Eddie knelt down and picked her up again.

"I'm going to bleed to death," she feared, her voice quivering in his embrace.

"Ain't gonna happen, sister."

Sheila bit her lip to stay awake. She buried her head in his chest, and they continued downhill. Pressed against his chest, the sound of his beating heart was amplified in her ear.

She drifted off and lost sense of time and place.

Her mind took her to a memory with her mother, before the wheelchair, when she was still healthy. They were making dinner together. Sheila was cutting vegetables and her mother was stirring the pot on the stove. There were no words spoken, didn't have to be, simply a quiet moment of mother and daughter working together.

Then Sheila was back in the hospital room watching as her mother's skin tone changed color, the image she couldn't get out of her mind, that transition to the other side.

Sheila wanted a daughter someday but was convinced she wasn't going to survive. She began to cry in Eddie's embrace, then let the tears flow.

She felt Eddie set her down again. "We made it," he said, gasping for air.

She squinted through tears to see the Gold Strike through the trees. All the lights were out and the parking lot was barren. Rising smoke behind the building reflected the fire's amber light. "Where is everybody?" she wondered aloud.

"Gone."

"The electricity is out," she said, scanning the darkened lodge for any sign of life.

"My car is around back," Eddie said.

"I don't get it," she said. "You'd think they would have come back for us."

"Don did."

"But he didn't return."

"Maybe the fire crew forced everyone to evacuate," he said.

"I don't get it."

"Maybe that fire truck we missed was sent for us. Let's go." Eddie picked her up again and Sheila could see he had newfound energy. Through the acrid smoke drifting eerily through the trees, he carried her down to the hotel.

CHAPTER
THIRTY-SEVEN

Eddie set Sheila down on a wooden bench in the lobby of the Gold Strike Lodge. He checked her wound. Blood had soaked her entire backside and his crude paper-towel bandage had all but dissolved. He found bath towels behind the counter and a pair of scissors. He cut her pullover top back to get to the wound and used bottled water to clean it, a quick fix for now.

He went into the bar and came back with a bottle of vodka.

"What are you doing?"

"Sterilizing." Eddie gently poured it over the wound. He blotted the puncture with the white towels. The scent of vodka hit his nostrils and it made him crave a drink, just to set his mind right. "It may be crude, but it'll do the trick for now. You okay?"

"I'm really tired."

"Probably getting anemic." It appeared the wound had congealed and was not bleeding as much as before. "Hang in there. My car keys are up in my room. I'll get them and we'll get out of here."

"Hurry," she said.

Eddie could see tears in her eyes. "You'll be okay," he said.

She gave him a nod, more tears flowing.

"Hold on," he said then bounded up the stairs.

Eddie found his room in the darkened hallway. He grabbed the car keys off the bureau next to the bottle of scotch he'd shared with Sam Carver. This was too expensive a bottle to leave behind, but Eddie realized he couldn't carry both it and Sheila. He felt like he needed a drink so he took a moment to gulp straight from the bottle. The liquor burned his parched throat and he immediately regretted it. Surely Sheila would smell it on his breath. *What was I thinking?*

Self-loathing, he swigged another shot and tossed the bottle. *Fuck it.* He coughed as he moved through the darkened hallway, could see the fire engulfing the trees out the window.

At the top of the landing, Eddie could see Sheila had fallen from the bench. "Sheila!" he rushed down.

He stopped on the stairway midway. Diane, half of her face covered in blood, was standing in the lobby pulling the string of her bow back, about to release an arrow on Sheila. Instead she spun and aimed the weapon up at him.

"Diane, don't …"

There was a jolt.

Eddie knew he'd been hit, heard Sheila scream. He looked down at his belly but there was no shaft. *Where had it gone?* He staggered back to see the arrow stuck in the wooden banister behind him. Eddie realized that at such a short range the arrow must have gone straight through his body.

The next arrow struck him in the chest. He heard ribs crack.

Eddie fell forward and rolled down the stairs. He was trying to get up when Diane approached. She kicked him then went to pry the first arrow out of the banister. Enraged, Diane said, "Look at this disgusting place, innocents killed and stuffed for some kind of fucked-up amusement." She pressed her foot onto his chest and yanked the second arrow out. Fireworks of pain exploded in Eddie's head. Whiskey-tainted bile sprung up into his throat.

Diane stared down at him with a look of disgust.

* * *

Sheila stared at the pickax.

It was plain as day. It had been there hanging on the wall the entire time among the vintage mining tools that decorated the wood paneling, shovels, gold pans, crude lanterns—and a black iron pickax.

The rusty tool had a sharp point on one end and a flat chisel on the other.

With Diane's back to her, Sheila managed to climb to her feet. It was a struggle but she forced herself up. She *willed* it. Sheila then pried the pickax from the wall brackets. The thing was heavy. She decided the pointed end would work best and grasped the wooden handle.

Sheila knew she'd only have one shot. Raising it over her head was incredibly painful. She clenched her teeth, pushed through it.

Diane sensed Sheila behind her and turned around.

For a split second, Diane's eyes registered a look of confusion— then there was brief a glimmer of panic.

Sheila swung the tool down with all her might.

At impact, she felt the vibration through wooden handle—much like splitting a log, but this, this was the feel of a skull cracking.

Eddie saw Sheila behind Diane the second before she turned. He saw the pickax come down. When the ax sliced into the top of Diane's head, it made a hollow, crunching sound.

One last act of defiance, it took everything Sheila had, and she fell to her knees.

Diane cried out and staggered back. She managed to reach up and grab the embedded ax with both hands. Miraculously still on her feet, Diane staggered and twisted around in some sort of spastic dance, and then crumbled to the floor, writhing in misery, still clawing at the pickax.

Eddie lay back on the stairs, his blood covering his feet. The wave of nausea came on strong. Then he passed out.

All Sheila could think about was that she'd just killed again.

Last time it was the ballpoint pen. She'd signed her mother's life away. This time the weapon was a rusty ax. She could see the tool lodged into Diane's head and there was a look of shock on her face, and her were eyes crossed. Illuminated by firelight, Sheila could see Diane's skin turn ashen, just as her mother's had, and Tami's for that matter. The brink of death.

She watched as Diane crossed the threshold.

This is what I've done.

She felt a presence and raised her head, expecting to see the angel of death over her shoulder, the same celestial spirit that came for her mother. But nothing was there.

The raging fire was visible out the window, angrily licking the trees, the porch now aflame. She could hear the sound of windows breaking. Sheila could hardly move and wondered how much time she had before the structure was engulfed entirely. She'd surely burn to death.

Stuffed animal carcasses stared back at her.

This is hell. I'm in it now.

A swirling blur came over her before all went black.

CHAPTER
THIRTY-EIGHT

Eddie sprung awake to the thundering roar of the fire. The heat was unbearable, singeing his eyebrows. He lifted his head and could see the inferno was burning everything outside the lobby, support beams now falling. The flickering light from the flames cast strange shadows across Sheila's prone body.

Eddie hoped she was still alive.

He checked his stomach wounds and could feel the warmth of blood on his fingers. Eddie summoned the strength to get up and went for Sheila. He couldn't remember when he'd lost control of his bladder but it must have been when he passed out—his ravaged innards betraying him with every step.

It didn't matter.

She was unconscious, but he could still feel her pulse. "Let's go," Eddie said and pushed through the pain to pick Sheila up.

He felt something inside his stomach pop before he struggled to balance himself, piss, blood, and stomach acid running down his quivering legs.

Eddie got his bearings and headed for the door.

The image of John Wayne carrying Natalie Wood in *The Searchers* came to mind. He'd seen the John Ford classic many times, a tale of obsession, of redemption.

Outside he could feel the heat from the blaze so much stronger. The smoke burned his eyes and he could barely see. He heard glass breaking from exploding windows, turned back to see the raging fire behind him.

Keep going.

Eddie heard Sheila whimper. She opened her eyes to look at him. He couldn't make out the words she was saying but nodded as if he understood. He kept staggering forward.

Press on.

The fire truck came around the bend. Its windshield reflected the golden light of the blaze behind him. The truck's lights blinded Eddie and all was a wet blur.

The truck slowed and came to a stop as he squinted, blinded by the high beams. He heard the truck doors open and saw cloaked figures emerge in heavy fire gear. They came to him and he carefully passed Sheila off. "She's been shot," he said.

There was an ambulance behind the fire truck and his next sensation was being placed on a stretcher. They were tending to his wounds and asking questions. When Eddie couldn't move his legs, or make out what the men were saying, he realized his time was near.

He wasn't afraid.

He'd given life his best shot.

No regrets.

He figured he'd go out like he was in the final reel of a Bogart movie or a Western. He didn't get the girl, wasn't supposed to—the gunfighters, gangsters, and private eyes never do. But he'd saved her life.

Love doesn't need to be returned to be real, does it?

Eddie saw the light, a warm and inviting place. It was someplace safe and welcoming. He was standing at the threshold. Eddie let himself go.

CHAPTER THIRTY-NINE

Sheila awoke in the hospital and wondered how she got there. She could only remember snippets of what happened—Eddie carrying her from the fire, the banks of fluorescent lights on the ceiling of the ambulance. Then she had images of the hospital and surgeons behind masks who worked above her.

Then there was a deep sleep without dreams.

Now she was awake, incredibly thirsty, and only after the nurse poured her a paper Dixie cup of water from a small plastic pitcher was she able to speak. "Where am I?"

"Riverside Medical," the nurse, a no-nonsense woman in her fifties with short hair, said. She marked something on the chart.

Sheila noticed there were tubes connected to her arm and bandages around her chest. They had put her in a green hospital gown. "What happened?" she asked the caregiver.

"You've been shot and lost a lot of blood."

"Where's Eddie?"

"Who?"

"The one I was with."

"I don't know what you're talking about."

"Sure you do. He and I ... the fire ..."

"Let me look into it," she said, set the clipboard down, and left the room.

When the nurse returned she was with a doctor, a dark-skinned man younger than Sheila, probably Indian or Pakistani, she figured. He glanced at the displays of the various machines she was connected to before asking, "How are you feeling, Sheila?"

"I need to know what happened to Eddie."

"He's in Intensive Care."

"I have to see him."

"I'm afraid that's not possible."

"Why not?"

"Only family are allowed to—"

"I'm his fiancée," she lied.

"Excuse me?"

"You have to let me see him. We're engaged ... that's family, right?" She could see wheels turning in the doctor's head and she hoped he wouldn't look down at her hand for an engagement ring.

He nodded and said, "Understand that he is not in stable condition and won't be able to—"

"I don't care. I need to see him." She stared at the doctor's dark eyes, pleading, "You don't understand, he saved my life."

"Let me see what I can do."

Twenty minutes later the nurses and techs released the wheels of her bed and rolled her out. They pushed her through the hallways and through automatic doors. They told her he'd be unconscious and to prepare her expectations. That didn't matter. Sheila needed to see him.

They wheeled her into his room and up beside his bed.

She could see he was intubated with a tube in his mouth and a machine automating his breathing. He shook slightly. For a second she thought he might wake up but then realized the movements were involuntary—his body fighting a battle somewhere deep inside.

Sheila sat up. "Eddie?" She reached out and took his hand. It was cold but there was warmth when she squeezed. She could see a hint of rosy color in his face. *Good. Stay that way.*

"Hey, Eddie," she said, "It's me, Sheila." She squeezed even harder, thought she felt a response, some movement there but wasn't sure. She hoped so. "I really need you, Eddie, so hang on, buddy," Sheila said, tears wetting her eyes, hoping he could hear. "All of us bottom feeders … we need to stick together."

Sheila studied the color of his skin.

Sheila would be there for him. She wouldn't let this life slip away.

ACKNOWLEDGMENTS

I owe a debt of gratitude to many who have played a role in bringing this book to life.

Thanks to the incredibly talented editor Peggy Hageman and everyone at Blackstone Publishing including Rick Bleiweiss, Josh Stanton, Josie McKenzie, Lauren Maturo, Megan Wahrenbrock, and Kathryn G. English, who designed an awesome book cover.

Big thanks to my agent Peter Rubie of FinePrint Literary Management.

A nod to early readers including Paul Marashlian and my writers group, known as the Oxnardians, especially Jonathan Beggs, who encouraged me to write from experience.

A big thanks to my film & TV collaborators from over the years, including Steve Jankowski, Neal Brown, Lawrence Maddox, Robert Eber, Brent White, Steven M. Blasini, Jason Zimmerman, and Sonny Carl Davis.

My deepest, heartfelt thanks to my wife and sounding board, Jennifer, for all of her love, support, and encouragement.